Adrienne Blinked, Then Blinked Again

She knew her eyes were open, but she could see nothing; everything was a silver-white void.

Seconds later the opaque screen before her was replaced by a face. The features were in shadow, but they appeared to be human.

Then she noticed a startling difference. There was a decidedly green cast to the skin.

Renewed terror gripped her, and a frightened cry escaped her dry lips as she made note of something even more unnatural: the man—the creature—had one clear-blue eye and one that was shimmering emerald green!

And his hair, it was dark and . . . slimy. The shiny strands glowed with green highlights.

She hadn't been dreaming at all. She had fainted to escape the inevitable, but now she was awake and in the clutches of a being from another planet.

Dear Reader:

SILHOUETTE DESIRE is an exciting new line of contemporary romances from Silhouette Books. During the past year, many Silhouette readers have written in telling us what other types of stories they'd like to read from Silhouette, and we've kept these comments and suggestions in mind in developing SILHOUETTE DESIRE.

DESIREs feature all of the elements you like to see in a romance, plus a more sensual, provocative story. So if you want to experience all the excitement, passion and joy of falling in love, then SILHOUETTE DESIRE is for you.

For more details write to:

Jane Nicholls
Silhouette Books
PO Box 236
Thornton Road
Croydon
Surrey CR9 3RU

JANET JOYCE
Out of This World

Silhouette Desire

Originally Published by Silhouette Books
division of
Harlequin Enterprises Ltd.

First published in Great Britain 1986
by Silhouette Books, 15–16 Brook's Mews, London W1A 1DR

© Janet Bieber and Joyce Thies 1986

Silhouette, Silhouette Desire and Colophon are Trade Marks of Harlequin Enterprises B.V.

ISBN 0 373 50395 4

22–0786

Printed and bound in Great Britain by
Cox & Wyman Ltd, Reading

JANET JOYCE

resides in Ohio and is happily married to the man who swept her off her feet as a college coed; she admits that her own romance is what prompted her writing career. She and her family like camping, traveling and are avid fans of college football. She is an accomplished pianist, enjoys composing her own lyrics and reads voraciously, especially the romances she loves.

Other Silhouette Books by Janet Joyce

Silhouette Desire

Winter Lady
Man of the House
Man of Glory
Controlling Interest
Run to Gold
Rare Breed
Out of the Shadows

*For further information about
Silhouette Books please write to:*

Jane Nicholls
Silhouette Books
PO Box 236
Thornton Road
Croydon
Surrey CR9 3RU

One

In the ruins of Los Angeles, a group of terrified survivors huddled in a small church. The sounds of destruction drew ever nearer. All was lost until suddenly an eerie silence dropped over the city. The alien machines had plummeted to earth, their creatures struck down by human germs for which they had no immunity.

Adrienne Castle gave a sigh of satisfaction as the movie credits rolled. H. G. Wells's *War of the Worlds* was truly a classic! Slinging the strap of her purse over her shoulder, she stood up and edged along the row of empty seats. Her feet crunched on the stale popcorn that covered the floor as she gained the aisle. When her heel caught in the frayed carpet and she nearly fell to her knees, she scolded herself for trying to vacate the ancient theater before the house lights had been turned up.

She was just too impatient. Impatient and impetuous—that was how her family described her, and those traits had always been her downfall. She hated to admit it but in this case her family was right.

Only someone who never planned ahead would have flown off to Pittsburgh, rented a car and driven into a remote region of the Alleghenies without making sure of what awaited her at the end of her journey. Thank God, she'd finally been able to find a decent restaurant and this decrepit movie house to wile away the long evening.

Even though she would have preferred doing something more constructive with her time, Adrienne had thoroughly enjoyed the double feature. Being able to see *The Day the Earth Stood Still* and *War of the Worlds* at one sitting was the ultimate treat for a science fiction buff like herself. She must have seen the eight-foot-tall robot, Gort, step from his huge flying saucer a hundred times but it still chilled her to the marrow.

Michael Rennie's portrayal of Klaatu, the sensitive representative of the Planetary Federation, never failed to move her. His warning to the people of Earth was still timely; mankind's rampant aggressiveness was as great a threat today as it had been in 1951 when *The Day the Earth Stood Still* was released.

For sheer terror, however, one couldn't beat *War of the Worlds*. The three-fingered Martians that pulverized humans with their heat beams showed H. G. Wells's mastery of monsters. From shaggy white degenerates with glowing eyes in *Time Machine* to the revolting, one-eyed, bulbous-headed creatures she'd just seen, Wells had no equal. To her way of thinking, none of the current film releases could compare with the old classics.

At last, the house lights came on and Adrienne no longer had difficulty finding her way to the theater exit. She certainly didn't have to fight the crowds, she thought, and giggled to herself. An eighty-year-old usher and a scattering of rosy-lipped teenagers were the only other occupants of the rundown movie house.

Adrienne didn't even try to hide her smile as she walked to the exit door. Teenagers were the same all over, no matter the year or the location. Scary movies and dark theaters provided the perfect setting for some serious necking. She wished she were leaving the place under the protective arm of a big, strong male. She might be twenty-four years old and an independent career woman, but creepy movies always had the same effect on her—she was scared stiff!

The fine blond hairs at the back of her neck were still standing on end as she pushed through the exit. The blast of wind that hit her as she stepped out onto the street almost lifted her one-hundred-pound body off the ground. She shivered, thinking the frigid wind felt like the cold fingers of aliens investigating her flesh. Every dark shadow she passed seemed to hold a threatening presence, and she couldn't get to her car fast enough.

These fearful moments and the nightmares that would probably follow were the price Adrienne had to pay whenever she indulged herself like this. Films starring Godzilla or any of his slimy, reptilian friends were science fiction, too, but they were comedies compared to the spine-chilling possibility of alien invasion. A firm believer in the existence of life on other planets, Adrienne was a patsy for the suggestions put forth in science fiction films like the ones she'd just viewed.

"I must be a masochist," she mumbled, "or out of my mind." Her trembling fingers fumbled with her car keys as she unlocked the small, gray Chevette she'd rented the day before. Anyone who repeatedly—eagerly—subjected themselves to terror had to be crazy.

Of course going to the double feature wasn't the only proof of her insanity, she admitted nervously, her large brown eyes surveying the deserted area. Her willy-nilly trip to the mountains in search of a reclusive toy inventor was further testimony that she wasn't playing with a full deck. If she had any sense at all, she'd still be sharing her spring vacation with her eldest sister. Rosie's family lived on the sugar-white beaches of Pensacola, Florida.

Once safely inside the car, Adrienne quickly locked all the doors, started the engine and pulled out onto the empty street. My sisters may be right. Perhaps I do need a keeper, she acknowledged grudgingly to herself while waiting impatiently for a traffic light to turn green.

Her rational side kept reminding her that the films were fiction but... Just in case, she was ready to floor the accelerator and make a fast getaway. Who knew what lurked in the shadows of the dark streets of Elkins, West Virginia?

Finally, the light changed and she proceeded through the small town, wishing she were in the middle of rush hour traffic back in Minneapolis. People and daylight always seemed to add an element of security, but this burg had no such safeguards at the moment. "I should know better than to go to movies like that alone at night," she announced, wishing there were someone else in the car to help break the ominous silence that seemed to close in on her.

Back home, she would have bribed one of her five older sisters or a friend to accompany her to the show. As a child, she had constantly plagued her family to take her to the Saturday matinees that came to their local theater—even if it had meant lying to them about the bad dreams she'd suffered afterward. No, she'd insisted stubbornly. The one-eyed monsters, radiation guns and man-eating vegetables depicted on the screen hadn't rattled her. Besides, being scared silly was the best part of going to the movies and she could never understand other people's reluctance to share in the bloodcurdling thrills.

Since it was well past ten o'clock on a weeknight, there was little traffic or activity on Elkins's main thoroughfare. Adrienne could only imagine what awaited her in Rocky Bottom Hollow, the less than one-horse town where she was staying. She hoped they hadn't rolled up the sidewalks and turned off the streetlights before she got back to that ramshackle row of cabins they called a motor court.

"What am I thinking?" she commented aloud. "There aren't any sidewalks or streetlights there." Rocky Bottom Hollow was merely a cluster of buildings at the crossing of two county roads, not large enough to qualify even as a village. If she'd blinked on the way into town, she might have missed it.

Before checking in at the Royal Pine Motel, Adrienne had erroneously assumed that that sort of establishment had gone the way of the Edsel and the hoola hoop. Living in the back of beyond, the owner of her rustic accommodations didn't appear to know that the rest of the world had progressed into the twentieth century. To a person used to modern conveniences, the Royal Pine was a royal pain.

It had no television, no bathtub, and a shower head that hung down from the ceiling above the large circular drain in the cement floor of the bathroom. There wasn't any room service since there wasn't any phone. Then again, who was there to call? Worse yet, there wasn't a golden arch or a white castle for as far as the eye could see.

"What do people do when they have a burger attack?" she inquired of the cement bridge across the highway. "How can they stand living somewhere that doesn't have pizza delivery? It's un-American."

Living in such isolation was totally foreign to her. As the youngest of six girls, she'd never been without company while growing up. The big old house where her parents still lived had been full of people. "Just let me know at income tax time how many I'm supposed to declare," had been his standing joke at meals, when her father would take a head count of those assembled around the long table. Rarely had the number been confined to eight, and he'd teased her mother that she'd sneaked some extras into the fold when he wasn't looking.

Like her parent's home, Adrienne's apartment was often as crowded as a bus depot, with friends and relatives passing through at all hours. The lease claimed she was the sole occupant but that was infrequently the case. If she wasn't tripping over one of her twelve nieces or nephews, she was providing temporary shelter for some down-on-her-luck friend.

Those few times she found herself alone in the apartment, the thin walls let her hear the dozens of people living with her in the complex. How many times had she wished for total silence? To have only herself for company? That was what she had to look forward to back at the Royal Pine, but tonight she would have been happy to stay in a room that was firmly connected to others, especially if her fellow occupants were noisy merrymakers. Right now, a huge, high-rise hotel filled with overly friendly conventioneers sounded like heaven. Unfortunately, absolute privacy was what the Royal Pine promised its patrons, and that was what they got.

"I'll probably spend the night huddled under the covers with all the lights on," she muttered as she fiddled with the radio dials on the dash, desperately trying to find a station that played cheerful music.

Less than ten minutes later, she was driving through a black tunnel of towering pines. Humming along with the country and western tune broadcast by a station in Wheeling, she tried to keep her thoughts off her fears and recall the directions she'd been given to Elkins. According to Hattie May Carson, the wizened proprietress of the Royal Pine, all she had to do was reverse the order of the landmarks for the return trip. She'd successfully maneuvered the winding mountain roads hours before; surely she could do it again.

But it had been daylight the first time she'd taken this route and now it was pitch black. Why was it that every time she had to drive in unfamiliar territory at night, the moon and stars went on vacation? She was still on Route 92 and the first turnoff would be marked. She saw it. U.S. Highway 250. So far, so good. The tricky part was coming up soon and she tried to remember Hattie's exact words.

"Take a left by Clover Rock, cain't miss that," Hattie May had assured, her faded blue eyes squinting as if she were picturing the landmark. "Then go on a piece 'till you spy two ol' crooked trees. That's where you'll find the road down to the main highway. Three or so switchbacks and you'll be on it fer sure."

Those switchbacks had been easy enough to figure out on the descent down the western slope of the Allegheny Mountains, in the daylight. Now Adrienne slowed and leaned forward, straining her eyes to see through the pervading darkness. A narrow road leading off the highway looked familiar and she turned onto it. After a couple more turns, she started watching for the two crooked trees Hattie May had mentioned.

A short while later, when the landmark still hadn't come into view, another female voice began ringing in her ears. Rosie's opinion of her impromptu trip repeated itself. "If I can't talk you out of this wild-goose chase, promise to call me the instant you know where you'll be staying. At least I'll know where to go to claim the body."

Adrienne had stubbornly informed her overprotective sister that she was a mature adult and perfectly capable of taking care of herself. That hadn't been a successful way to justify her journey so she'd tried another. Remaining calm, she'd reminded Rosie that she was the Assistant Director of Marketing for Lang Manufacturing and as such, had a responsibility to the company to investigate new talent.

"If the president of Lang has confidence in me, I don't see why my own sister doesn't," Adrienne had said, trying to hold her temper.

"Mr. Lang hasn't known you all your life," Rosie had scoffed. "Besides, Lang's a pretty small company."

"Small but growing fast," Adrienne had defended hotly. "And it'll be a major company if I can get the rights to those talking action figures and that remote controlled spaceship."

The child in her, never far from the surface, bubbled up. "Think of it, Rosie. It's like being the captain of a real spaceship. You can just zoom in, hover over the landing party and whisk your stranded crew away to safety. Those little men jump right into the spaceship from as far as three feet away. It's incredible!"

Then as if she'd flipped a switch inside herself, Adrienne had come back from her space adventure and planted both feet firmly on the ground. The adult Adrienne—the successful businesswoman—took over. "I don't know why somebody hadn't come up with this idea before. It's all so simple, really, and I think it'll be cost-effective for both the manufacturer and the consumer."

Settling down into the details of it, she'd gone on to explain how the toy worked. "It functions on the same principle as a model airplane and uses an electromagnet for the 'beaming up.' By its very simplicity, it's the creation of a genius. I have to meet this Sloan character. A mind like his must be capable of cooking up all kinds of wonderful toys and I want to have first claim on them.

"If I can convince him to sell me the rights to his inventions, Lang can manufacture and market an entire line of toys that will sell like hotcakes. I wasn't wrong on last year's Kids'n Roo and I'm even more excited about this. That man's flying saucer will be an even bigger hit."

The promotion of the lovable stuffed kangaroo with its pouch full of cuddly "roo" babies had been her greatest achievement thus far. Though this new find would appeal to a different market, she was sure the mini spacemen and their alien counterparts would boost both her career and Lang Manufacturing's sales like a rocket. If their creator accepted her proposal, Lang stood to make millions.

Adrienne had already placed a call to her boss, Ted Erwin. Her enthusiastic description of the toy had won him over within minutes and he'd given her the authority to make an offer to the toy maker. Adrienne was determined to make sure that every child in America would soon be able to beam action figures aboard their very own spaceship.

She was grateful for the lucky star that had been shining over her head the day her nephew, Paul, had introduced her to his best friend, Kenny Robinson. Since Rosie had had to spend the day at the orthodontist so that her daughters could be fitted for braces, Adrienne had volunteered to take the other three children, along with Kenny, to the beach.

While Adrienne stretched out on a towel to rid herself of her Minnesota pallor, Kenny had shown her the present he'd just received from his Dad's buddy, Kendrick Sloan. Noting Adrienne's interest, the boy had proudly relayed the information that he'd been named after the ingenious designer of his space-age toys.

Upon further investigation, Adrienne had learned from Kenny's mother, Phyllis, that Kendrick Sloan had once saved her husband's life. Greg Robinson, a naval pilot, had been rescued from his downed aircraft by Sloan, an air force pararescueman. Since Pensacola Naval Air Station and Eglin Air Force Base were not far apart, the two men had become friends. Apparently, Greg thought so highly of Sloan that he'd named his son after him.

During the visit Adrienne had been shown a collection of rockets, Martian monsters and *Star Wars* lightsabers Sloan had designed. She'd wanted to hop in the nearest car and race over to Eglin in order to meet their creator but had been told he'd been forced to retire from pararescue three years earlier.

According to Phyllis, Kendrick Sloan had been severely injured in an explosion on a distressed oil freighter and been hospitalized for many months. To help pass the time during his long rehabilitation, Sloan had started making toys. The spaceship and crew were the latest in a vast array of playthings Sloan had sent to his namesake.

The man now lived atop an isolated mountain in West Virginia, had either an unlisted number or no telephone and could be reached only through a post office box number. Unwilling to waste time on a lengthy exchange of correspondence, Adrienne had elected to drop everything and track the man down. Rosie had done everything in her power to talk Adrienne out of it but she had been adamant. As far as she was concerned, this was a career opportunity she could not afford to pass up.

Unimpressed by Adrienne's logic, Rosie had admonished sternly, "Honestly, Addie, I can't imagine what I'm going to tell Mother if she calls to find out how you're enjoying your vacation. If I say you went off half-cocked to visit some strange recluse in the Appalachians, she'll have my head. After all the trouble you've managed to get yourself into over the years, one would hope you'd have learned to think before jumping into things.''

Rosie's maternal instincts had been fostered at their mother's knee. Rebecca Castle had expected the older children to help look after the younger ones and Rosie had taken that responsibility seriously. Ten years older than Adrienne, Rosie treated her irrepressible youngest sister as if she were a member of her own rambunctious brood.

The attitude of Pat Callahan, Rosie's big jovial husband, was little better. He was a career navy officer and he failed to see that Adrienne was older than the majority of sailors under his command.

"Princess Addie of the Castle," he'd called her in what had once seemed to Adrienne the most delightful of puns. That had been fifteen years ago when he'd been the dashing Annapolis midshipman who'd swept her oldest sister away in storybook romance style. But to Pat, Adrienne was still the kid sister she'd been when he and Rosie had married.

For that reason, Adrienne was thankful Pat had been at sea when she and Rosie had battled over the wisdom of this trip. She was sure he would have figured out some way to prevent her from going.

"Probably would have thrown me in the brig if all else failed," Adrienne judged fatalistically. "Or assigned two of his men to escort me."

She finally spotted the two crooked trees and turned onto a graveled road that seemed far more narrow, winding and bumpy than she remembered. The countryside appeared to have sprouted dozens of pairs of crooked trees. She began to think there would have been some merit in having a military escort. Sailors didn't get lost on the ocean; surely they could chart a course through the Alleghenies.

But then the navy relied on radar, which wasn't standard equipment in rented cars. She was on her own without even a compass to guide her and Mother Nature seemed to dislike her. Not only had the moon and stars been blacked out, but a heavy fog was rolling in. A dense mist nestled in the hollows and blanketed the road, cutting visibility down to a few yards.

She'd never felt such relief as when she spotted Clover Rock and took what she assumed was the final cutoff to Rocky Bottom Hollow. The feeling was short-lived. A few miles down the road, Clover Rock reappeared in her rear-view mirror. Suddenly she realized that *every* road in West Virginia sported a selection of clover rocks and crooked trees.

She no longer had any doubt that she was thoroughly and irretrievably lost. She was a trembling mass of nerves. Alone, unarmed, helpless, she drove down a dark road to nowhere.

Her earlier fears took on new life. The sinister mountains leaned in on her. Her headlights seemed to glint off watchful eyes. It was as if she'd entered another dimension, the *Twilight Zone*, the perfect place for...

"Get a grip on yourself!" Adrienne scolded desperately, trying in vain to keep her imagination from running wild. She had definitely watched *Chiller Theater* once too often.

Abruptly the music from the radio disintegrated into static. Wasn't this usually the first sign of an imminent alien invasion? Again she forced her unsettling thoughts away. There was a perfectly logical explanation for this. Transmission had been blocked by the dips and hollows of the foothills. Once she was out of them, Tammy Wynette would be singing "Stand By Your Man" once again.

To fortify her courage, Adrienne began whistling a happy tune from *The King and I*, thankful that her mother had dragged her to that delightful musical. With renewed bravery, she forged on. Every road had a purpose and this one would eventually lead her somewhere.

It did. A slatted wooden gate loomed up out of the mist and she had to slam on the brakes to avoid crashing into it. "Hell's bells!" she howled in dismay.

She couldn't go forward and doubted she could turn around. The granite stone of the mountain hemmed her in on one side and the other side of the road dropped away into darkness. She didn't dare back up for fear of veering off into the void.

There was only one solution, disagreeable though it might be. She, five feet of defenseless terror, had to step out into the unknown and try to determine what lay ahead. The gate was either a warning of upcoming hazards or the entrance to private property. She prayed it was the latter and that some kindly human resided not far away.

Mountain folk were reputed to be a friendly lot, she reminded herself, as she groped in the glove compartment for a flashlight and found nothing. She'd have to leave the headlights on to make out whatever lay beyond the gate. Crossing her fingers, she stepped out of the car.

Step by faltering step, she approached the gate. If her hair was turning white from fear, she thought, at least it didn't have far to go from its original light yellow. She giggled nervously. What difference did hair make? Fear was fear.

The wind blew several pale gold strands across her face but she couldn't tell if the color had faded any. In the moonlight, it looked silvery. Moving against the resistance of her knocking knees, keeping a firm lookout for any signs of danger, she finally reached her goal.

Keep Out! This Is Private Property, read the crudely painted sign that dangled from the top slat of the gate. It looked like a welcome mat to her. Someone with hands had painted it. Someone who knew how to spell had composed the hostile message. She could deal with some ordinary down-to-earth hostility. It was the extraordinary, the extraterrestrial she wanted to avoid at all costs.

The latch was covered with some very common looking rust and Adrienne took heart. She was just being fanciful. She peered down the road and saw no reason not to open the gate and continue onward.

She had just convinced herself she had nothing more to worry about when she heard a strange rustling sound above her. Looking up, she saw a weird glow. Paralyzed, afraid to move or breathe, Adrienne watched as something right out of *War of the Worlds* descended from the heavens.

This was it! After all these years, she was finally going to have a "close encounter of the third kind." The reality was not nearly as thrilling or uplifting as had been conveyed on film. She did not hear the comforting five-note musical sentence that signaled the coming of the mother ship, but a powerful whir hovering malevolently overhead.

A beam of blue-white light shone down, outlining her quaking figure in stark relief against the darkness. Her mouth opened but the scream was trapped in her throat just as she was trapped by the brilliant heat ray. Her every nerve shouted a warning. Soon she would be the helpless subject of one of those alien experiments reported in the *National Enquirer*. She just knew it.

She couldn't move. She must be rooted in place by the force field surrounding her. Incapable of being anything but a mute witness, Adrienne stared as the glow in the sky took form. Her eyes widened in horror as what looked like a gigantic, foil-wrapped baked potato landed on the ground nearby. The creature stood only a few yards away from her and it was immediately aware of her presence.

Giving off a strange beeping sound, it moved slowly toward her. Adrienne relinquished her breath. The glowing thing was trying to communicate with her but she was sure it wasn't sending a friendly message. If she didn't get away to the safety of her car, she might never see earth again.

Fighting her way out of the restraining beam, she ran for her life. In her heedless flight she tripped over a root and pitched forward. She landed face down in the gravel, the impact of the fall knocking the wind out of her lungs.

She heard heavy footfalls coming nearer and nearer. Terror took the last bit of air from her body and permeated every muscle and nerve. Then as the scaly, alien fingers clasped her shoulder, consciousness fled, and she gave herself up to her fate.

Two

_____

Damn! Damn and double damn!'' Kendrick Sloan swore, his voice resounding hollowly within the confines of his bubble helmet. "Talk about major foul-ups.'' He pulled off his bulky gloves and tossed them down beside the unconscious woman. He wished heartily that she wasn't there.

Hours of planning had gone into tonight's test. He'd checked and double-checked everything that could possibly go wrong. Never once had he expected some fool woman to be standing smack-dab in the middle of his secret landing site. He'd chosen the spot specifically because of the overhanging trees and steep ravines. He'd wanted to make it as difficult as possible for the second chopper to locate him.

Instead, the dense cover had hidden the woman's car until it was too late. By the time her headlights had been spotted, he'd already begun his descent from the

helicopter. Someplace along the line there'd been a
serious breakdown in his security.

He would have liked nothing better than to strap his
harness back on and be hoisted aboard the copter, but
his old training died hard. He couldn't leave an apparently injured person alone in the middle of nowhere—especially when he no doubt had been the
cause of her injury. Sighing in resignation, he shut off
the beep of the homing device in his suit and sank to
his knees. He pressed his fingers to the side of the
woman's neck, checking for a pulse.

It was strong but too rapid. She was in shock. Before he could do anything about that, he had to make
certain she'd sustained no other damage from the
nasty fall she'd just taken. With sure fingers he traced
her small form, unconsciously gathering more information than he required. He didn't find any broken
bones or serious wounds, but some delightful shapes
and soft curves.

Gently, he rolled the petite woman onto her back
and saw an angelic face marred only by a few scratches
and smudges of mud. Her complexion was as smooth
and light as alabaster, her nose small with an impu-
dent tilt. Her mouth looked like the pink petals of a
spring flower waiting for the kiss of rain.

Out of nowhere came a desire to bestow that kiss,
but Kendrick pushed it aside. This was definitely not
the time or place to indulge in such prurient urges. Her
life and the secrecy of his mission were at stake.

Still, he couldn't stop himself from making a lingering study of her face. She was a knockout. Though
her hair was a shimmering golden blond, her lashes
were dark and lush, lying like sable fans against her

soft skin. With a little water those delicate features would be none the worse for wear.

Having assured himself that she needed no other first aid, he was free to treat her for shock. The first order of business was to elevate her legs. He removed his helmet and thrust it beneath a pair of dainty feet clad in expensive loafers. Next, he unbuttoned a silky pink blouse, then unclasped a flimsy lace bra. He groaned and resisted the temptation to expose more of the creamy white breasts he'd released from confinement.

Ignoring his masculine response to undressing one hell of a good-looking woman, he undid the snap on her designer jeans and lowered the zipper a couple of inches. With nothing left to constrict her breathing, he had only to control his own and to keep her warm. Discarding several intimate ideas for warming her up, he fell back reluctantly on the standard method.

Getting to his feet, he slipped out of his backpack, opened it up and pulled out a silver sheet. Swiftly unfolding the thermal covering, he lowered it over the supine beauty and tucked it securely around her. Now what? What the devil was he going to do with her?

Hoping his pilot might have a solution in mind, he activated the radio in his experimental flight suit and barked into the transceiver, "Falling Star to Ranger One. Come in, Ranger One."

He knew that the helicopter hovering not too far above the treetops had maintained visual contact. It followed that everyone on the team had now been advised that their mission was scrubbed. When he got no answer to his transmission, Kendrick realized that advice would not be coming from above. He swore with annoyance then threw protocol out the window.

"Damn it, Hank! Say something! I know you can hear me. We can't leave her here and we sure as hell can't take her with us."

A spurt of static was followed by a gruff chortle, then Hank Comstock's booming voice crackled with amusement. "You're on your own, buddy. You're supposed to be the expert in tight situations. Unless you want us to airlift her to a hospital, we should make ourselves scarce. We were supposed to be in and out of here like a hot knife through butter."

Kendrick relayed a suitably coarse rejoinder then ordered the copter to stay put until he'd checked out the woman's car. Without compunction, he rifled the contents of the purse he found on the front seat. This woman who had fouled their plans wore pink lipstick and a light floral perfume, and loved candy. In her wallet he found more than five hundred dollars in cash, enough credit cards to outfit Queen Elizabeth, and at least a dozen children's pictures.

He estimated that she was in her early twenties. With those few years and her trim body, she couldn't be the mother of that brood. So what was she doing with all those pictures? Maybe she was a teacher. If that were the case, things had changed since he'd gone to school. Maybe he'd have paid more attention in class if he'd had a looker like her for a teacher.

A Minnesota driver's license identified her as Adrienne Castle and the picture matched the real thing. What was a gorgeous woman from Minnesota doing wandering around in the middle of the night on a deserted back road in West Virginia? He doubted she had any connection with the locals. She had to be lost.

According to the rental agreement he found, she'd picked up the car in Pittsburgh the day before. His brows rose as he extracted a key ring. Why on earth would she be staying at the Royal Pine Motel?

So she wasn't just passing through. She, a woman who looked as if she'd just stepped out of *Glamour* magazine, was actually staying at that run-down place in Rocky Bottom Hollow. Who the devil was she? Somebody's runaway wife? A spoiled heiress out for a lark? Or did she have other business in the area? Business that concerned him?

Reluctantly, he made his decision. He'd put her in the car and take her back to the Royal Pine. With any luck, the fear that had caused her to faint would keep her unconscious for a while longer. He might be able to get her back to the cabin and disappear before she woke up. Maybe she'd scratch the whole thing off as a bad dream. He signaled the copter, then put his plan into motion.

Adrienne blinked then blinked again. She knew her eyes were open but she could see nothing. She could feel a lumpy surface beneath her but that was the only thing her numbed brain would register. All else was a silver-white void.

Seconds later, the opaque screen before her eyes was replaced by a face. The features were in shadow yet they appeared to be human. Then she noted a startling difference. There was a decidedly green cast to the skin. Renewed terror gripped her and a frightened mew escaped her dry lips as she focused on something even more unnatural. The man, the creature, whatever it was, had one clear blue eye and one that was a shimmering emerald green.

And his hair, it was dark and...slimy. The shiny strands glowed with green highlights. She hadn't been dreaming at all. She had fainted to escape it, but now she was awake and in the clutches of a being from another world.

Other realizations came to her all at once. Her blouse was unbuttoned and a narrow strip of her bare skin was exposed from neck to waist. She could feel the unclasped cups of her bra crushed beneath her limp arms. Gulping down a gigantic lump of fear, she lifted her hand to her stomach and covered the V-shaped gap made by her unfastened jeans.

All those crazy articles she'd read about people who had been taken aboard UFO's and examined by creatures from other planets had been true. She was now a victim of such an examination and if she lived to tell the tale, it would cause a brief sensation then be dismissed as the ravings of a lunatic. She could see the headlines now, "SciFi Buff Snatched By Starmen." Never again would she question the outlandish stories she read in the papers.

"Please. Let me go," she begged as tears of fright gathered in her huge brown eyes. "I don't want to go to another planet. Please take me back. Take me back to earth."

Mouth gaping in horror, she watched as the blurred humanlike face came closer, lowered to within an inch of her own. She closed her eyes to escape the ghastly sight. She wasn't sure if she was hearing the deep velvet voice, or if it came to her through some sort of telepathy. "You are back," it said. "Sleep now. You have nothing to worry about."

Sleep! Her mind screamed. How can I sleep when this visitation might have some horrible results? If this green-faced monster kissed her, would she be giving birth to a lizard nine months from now?

"No, no," she whimpered. "I don't want your baby."

She heard a muffled sound. Was it a laugh? Did aliens have a sense of humor? Maybe the sound was simply the bestial glee of a creature bent on pigging out on human flesh.

"Please, don't hurt me," she babbled hysterically, refusing to open her eyes and view her unearthly assailant.

"I promise. This won't hurt a bit," it assured her as a soothing pressure was applied to her lips.

Adrienne wanted to fight, yet at the first touch of its mouth upon hers, she relaxed and allowed herself to sag with the lethargy that immobilized her body. It was as if the kiss had the power to close out her consciousness—the exact opposite of the effect of the prince's kiss in *Sleeping Beauty*. Her last clear thought was that the creature's lips were surprisingly warm and gentle.

Her nostrils picked up the scent of nighttime breezes on its skin. Its breath was not foul but remarkably sweet. If she hadn't known what was kissing her, she might have enjoyed it. Perhaps no harm would come of this after all.

"How did an outsider get through your security?" Tanner Gwinnett, Aerospace's security officer, inquired shortly, a tight expression on his face.

Gwinnett was past forty, came barely to Kendrick's shoulder and was definitely overweight, but he still had a commanding presence. "Aerospace is paying you a fortune for that flight suit and we can't afford any security leaks. We've got to make sure tonight's fiasco won't be repeated and hasn't backfired right in our faces.''

Kendrick acknowledged Gwinnett's concern but still didn't like what the older man was proposing. Although he knew next to nothing about her, Kendrick's instincts told him that Adrienne Castle wasn't the type to be involved in industrial espionage. She was too... Too what? Beautiful? Young? Feminine?

Kendrick's black brows knit in a frown. Those were exactly the traits his competitors might have concluded were necessary in his case. Adrienne Castle was the perfect choice to infiltrate his organization, get to him. If she were a spy he had to give her credit for quick thinking and extraordinary acting ability.

Her fright had been real. He didn't doubt that. Nobody could fake a rapid pulse. But had it been because she'd thought he was some space invader, or because she'd been discovered in the act of spying? The gibberish she'd spouted might have been a ploy to throw him off.

Why she would have chosen that particular tack he couldn't guess, except that he probably did look a bit like some creature from another world when he dropped down in that suit, glowing in the dark. But, if she'd invented that pose, would she have been able to call it up in a semiconscious state? That seemed unlikely, especially once the effect of the sedative started to take hold.

If Gwinnett's assessment of the incident were on target, and someone had checked into his background, they could very well have concluded that he was a lonely man, ripe for the picking. How long had it been since he'd had any female companionship?

After tonight, he knew the answer to that one—much too long! This celibate life was affecting his reason.

Even if he hadn't been a prime candidate for some feminine attention, Adrienne Castle would have made a strong impression on him. His curiosity about her was overwhelming. If things had been different, he'd have followed up on that interest at the earliest possible opportunity. What man wouldn't want to get better acquainted with a woman who looked part angel and part imp?

That was the danger. It would be too easy to trust her, to tell her anything just to get her in bed. At a vulnerable moment, he might disclose things she shouldn't know.

In her motel room, he'd practically had to drag himself away from her bedside, from that kissable mouth, those beautiful breasts. He'd stolen one kiss, before the sedative he'd given her had taken effect, and it had been enough to make him want to engage in a full-scale robbery. It had been years since a woman had fostered that kind of lust in him.

Maybe it was those huge brown eyes, so out of place on a blonde. Or maybe it was that perfume of hers that had acted like an aphrodisiac. He hadn't been around a desirable woman for much too long.

Kendrick jumped guiltily when Gwinnett was forced to touch his arm in order to reclaim his attention. "Sorry," he grunted, trying to get his errant thoughts back on track. He brushed a rebellious lock of black hair off his forehead, then asked somewhat sheepishly, "You were saying?"

"I wasn't saying anything. I was asking if there's anything else you can tell me before I start my investigation?'' Gwinnett repeated the question he'd asked only seconds before, but this time more loudly.

Kendrick was more than happy to go over the last hour in his mind once again but this time he made a valiant attempt to be more scientific about it. He viewed the facts he'd discovered and finally remembered one that he hadn't yet relayed to the surly security man. ''Her card says she's an assistant marketing director for Lang Manufacturing. Ever heard of them?''

''Good God!'' Gwinnett swore. ''How stupid do they think we are?''

He pulled a walkie-talkie out of his suit pocket and barked a summons into the transmitter. To Kendrick he snarled, ''Now we know Trenton Industries is hot on our trail. Lang is a little-known subsidiary of theirs. Make no mistake, Clyde Trenton wants those designs of yours any way he can get them—''

His speech was interrupted by a garbled response from his walkie-talkie. ''Roger,'' Gwinnett answered. ''I'll be right there. We'll take off in ten minutes.''

Shortly thereafter, Kendrick found himself alone in the house. Gwinnett had promised to be back within the week, with a full report on Adrienne Castle. Kendrick was supposed to continue with his work. He was to reschedule the test that would prove his lightweight, nonflammable, radio-equipped flight suit could save the lives of hundreds of downed pilots.

Naturally, he was supposed to maintain the strictest security, but if the Castle woman tried to contact him, he was advised to string her along. Until Gwinnett had proof of her association with Trenton Industries, Aerospace Limited's fiercest and most ruthless competitor, they would let her go on thinking she was making some progress. That way, Trenton wouldn't feel the need to approach Kendrick from another angle.

The idea of stringing her along inspired some delicious fantasies in Kendrick's mind. If it meant there was a chance a few of them might actually happen, he almost hoped she was a spy. If she wanted to seduce him into revealing classified information, he was hers for the taking. He could even drop enough information to keep her interested, though naturally not enough to jeopardize the project. She might be disappointed in her espionage efforts but he'd guarantee her satisfaction in other areas.

As he mounted the suspended stairs to the loft, stripping off his clothes on the way, Kendrick's stubborn jawline was softened by a grin. When he'd first come up with the idea for the flight suit, he hadn't considered all the possible ramifications. If he'd known that a luscious blond spy might try to ply him with her wicked wiles, he would have retired from the air force long before the accident.

Naked, he strode across the polished, hardwood floor of his bedroom and into the large, connecting bath. He stepped into the glass-enclosed shower and turned on the cold water. He'd lived and worked alone for most of the last two and a half years, and tonight his body had given him a violent reminder of that fact. A frigid shower would take care of his present discomfort but he suspected he wasn't going to enjoy a good night's sleep.

Out of the shower, he stood shivering in front of the wide mirror. Critically, he surveyed his wet body. He wondered what Ms. Adrienne Castle would think of him if she saw him like this, instead of looking like

some weird creature from another planet. Would she
be repulsed by the scars that marred his legs and chest?
Would she beg him to let her go, as she'd done tonight?

Believing her truly terrified, he'd wanted to cradle
her in his arms and reassure her that he was human,
but logic told him the less said the better. The imaginative woman had feared that he'd been about to im-
pregnate her with extraterrestrial seed. If he'd stayed
any longer, he could have proved that her fears were
partially justified. He wanted her. Would she ever
want him?

Gritting his teeth, he turned away from the damn-
ing glass and grabbed for a towel. He could feel the
despondency waiting in ambush for him, but this time
he wouldn't be its willing victim. He didn't need a
woman invading his solitude, cluttering up his well-
ordered life. He had his work; he was involved in a
project that would save countless lives. Adrienne
Castle could just go peddle her desirable wares someplace else. Kendrick Sloan wouldn't be buying.

Drip. Drip. Drip!

Adrienne knew that sound should be familiar but
for some reason she couldn't place it. She snuggled
deeper into the warm nest of blankets until the infer-
nal noise managed to cut through and reach her slug-
gish brain. Somewhere a faucet was dripping. Faucet?
If she could hear a faucet then ...

Abruptly, Adrienne threw off the blankets and sat
up. It was broad daylight, and she seemed to be alone
in her room at the Royal Pine Motel. A bubble of
panic came up in her throat as she gingerly climbed
out of bed and sidestepped along the wall to the bath-

room. A faucet in the freestanding sink was dripping but there was no monster in sight, nor did the plastic shower curtain conceal an inhuman assailant.

Adrienne's relief lent her courage and within moments she'd looked under the bed, snatched open the closet door and swept aside the heavy curtains in front of both windows. She was alone and perfectly safe, she assured herself as she double-checked the locks on the windows. At last, she could relax and try to come to grips with what had happened to her during the night.

She was still wearing the clothes she'd had on then and they were proof that the terrifying episode had not been a product of her overactive imagination. Her blouse was unbuttoned, her jeans unfastened and she knew she hadn't done that herself. Her purse lay on the bed, her car keys on the bureau. The last time she'd seen them they'd been with her in the car. The car!

Almost running to the front window, she flattened herself against the wall and peeked out. The Chevette was parked in front of her cabin. But who had driven it there? Except for those brief moments when she'd opened her eyes to stare up into an alien face, she couldn't remember a thing from the time she'd fallen down on the back road until this morning. Had she been drugged?

For more than an hour, Adrienne struggled to maintain her sanity as she tried to recall every detail of the previous night. She took off all her clothes and looked for telltale marks on her body. Hadn't she read somewhere that alien examinations left bloodless wounds?

Finding none, she took a shower to erase the uneasy sensation that she'd been touched by alien hands. She stood under the warm water, soaping, rinsing and then soaping again, making sure she'd removed any foreign substances left on her skin. Finally satisfied that she was thoroughly cleansed, she carefully toweled herself dry.

To reinforce the feeling of competence, she put on what she called her "power suit". Armored in the tailored navy wool she felt much better. Firmly back in control, she meticulously searched every inch of the room but found no evidence of a visitation by an unworldly phenomenon.

With no visible proof that it had happened, who would ever believe her story? Even her own family would say she'd simply got carried away at the movies and had thought the ensuing nightmares were real. She'd already placed her duty call to Rosie while at dinner in Elkins. She'd assured her sister all was well but apparently that assessment had been made too soon. She could almost hear a second conversation.

"Rosie, I did get in trouble. I got picked up by a flying saucer and an alien kissed me."

"Sure kid," Rosie would answer. "Tell me another one. I stopped believing your stories the night you insisted the man in the moon came down from the sky and invited you back up for a visit."

But this time it had happened. It had! She'd seen a UFO, an alien, had a close encounter. She truly had!

She began to doubt her own judgment when she noticed the dark green shade on the bedside lamp and switched on the light. It gave the room a ghostly green glow, which would explain some of what she'd seen, if the light had been on when she'd awakened in the throes of a nightmare. Had it all been just an incredibly lifelike dream? Had the creature bending over her, kissing her, been a figment of her imagination?

But how could she have forgotten making the trip back to the motel, loosening her clothes and climbing into bed? She'd had nothing alcoholic to drink last night and as far as she knew, popcorn wasn't a hallucinogen.

She was positive she'd gotten lost, been forced to stop by a wooden gate across the road, and then...then she'd seen "it" descending from the sky. Somehow that *thing* had transported both her and her car back to the motel. If it could travel trillions of light-years through outer space then it could certainly do something that easy, couldn't it?

She asked herself the same questions over and over again but never came up with a satisfactory answer. In any event, she knew it would be a good long time before she'd go see another science fiction movie. And there were a few television programs that would no longer be on her list of prime viewing.

That in itself was a kind of proof that "something" had indeed happened to her. The burning curiosity she'd always had over what it might be like to witness a UFO landing and meet a visitor from another planet was permanently quenched. From now on, Steven Spielberg would just have to make do without her generous support.

Three

———

"Did you enjoy the picture show last night?" Hattie May Carson called across the yard to Adrienne.

"Very much," Adrienne called back, unwilling to elaborate. As far as she was concerned, last night could be written off as a bad dream. If she never thought about it, never talked about it, it would eventually seem as if it had never happened. "Have you ever heard of Kendrick Sloan, Mrs. Carson?"

"Hattie. Folks always call me Hattie," the woman corrected. "Sure I heard of Kendrick Sloan. He is new to these parts and not much gets past me," Hattie said as she gestured for Adrienne to join her on the front porch of her cabin. "Sloan bought the family farm off ol' Leander Hubbard. Guess it's goin' on three years since he took over the place."

Abruptly, Hattie's forehead furrowed into a web of fine lines and her long angular features locked in a scowl. "I told my boy, Billy Lee, to stay in the office. Weren't he there? I told him you'd be leavin' first thing this mornin'. Seems like city folks cain't take peace and quiet fer more'n a day."

"I'm not leaving, Mrs. Carson...Hattie," Adrienne stammered, pasting a bright smile on her face that she was determined would stay put. "I want to talk to you."

Adrienne firmly believed in the old adage that one could catch more flies with honey, and if she were going to hasten her return to civilization, she needed to locate Kendrick Sloan. Hattie's "boy"—a man who looked to be well past thirty—had been as close-mouthed as a clam. All she'd been able to get out of him was a plastic menu for a small diner located two miles down the road. Evidently, that was where patrons of the Royal Pine had their meals. Too bad she hadn't gone there last night instead of to Elkins.

"Billy Lee was reluctant to tell me much about Mr. Sloan, but he said you might be able to answer my questions," she continued politely. Actually the man hadn't said any such thing. When she'd asked if Mrs. Carson were available to speak to her, he'd nodded in the affirmative and pointed out the window to the cabin behind the office.

Hattie nodded and smiled, saying, "Yep, my boy don't find much use in talkin'," as if this trait delighted her.

Adrienne was pleased that her sarcastic rejoinder didn't make it off the tip of her tongue. Billy Lee Carson had a two word vocabulary, "Yep" and "Nope." But it wouldn't help her cause any to tell his proud mother that he had the looks and intelligence of a hound dog. With determination, she held the smile that kept threatening to curl into a grimace.

As she slowly picked her way through the animals that inhabited the sparse plot of grass in front of Hattie's weather-beaten log house, she tried to appear at ease. In a business suit and high heels, she found herself walking through a domesticated version of *Wild Kingdom*. Chicken, pigs, two goats and several dogs and cats watched her unsteady progress toward the porch. So far, this business trip had been a disaster and she had yet to see any sign that things were going to improve. "I'm hoping you can tell me how I might locate Mr. Sloan," she tossed out, jumping to one side as a large collie bared his teeth at her.

"S'pect I can at that," Hattie said sagely, rocking back and forth on a narrow wooden porch swing. She picked a large brown nut from the bowl in her lap and split it in half with a rusty nutcracker. She threw the shells over her shoulder to where a cluster of hens pecked at the husks scattered on the ground.

"I can tell you about that bunch on Hubbard's Mountain. For one thing, Leander works the land for Sloan, but it don't look like he gets any more out'n it now than he used to. It pays a body t'work more'n it does t'starve, but Leander ain't starvin' or workin' much either," Hattie went on. "His wife Dovie does all the cookin' and cleanin' but at least they stayed on in their own house and don't live in that funny lookin', fancified place Sloan has built for hi'self."

"Funny looking?" Adrienne queried as she reached the relative safety of the porch. She had to make room for herself amongst the paper sacks, clothing and newspapers piled up on an old metal chair.

"Never seen the like," Hattie admitted. The tight white bun on the top of her head dipped forward over her left brow as she bent down and lifted another handful of pecans from the opened gunny sack on the floor.

"Sorry I cain't stop my crackin' whilst I talk but Agnes Whisholden is comin' to make up some of her butterscotch buns this forenoon and if I ain't ready, she'll keep on a'goin'. She's gawdawful prideful over her recipes and don't give 'em out nohow. When she's ready to make you a batch of them buns, you'd best be prepared. Good manners just have to take a second seat to that mean-minded old woman."

"That's all right," Adrienne replied, relieved that she wouldn't have to stay very long. Last night, it had taken Hattie almost twenty minutes to relay the best route to Elkins. "Please go on with your work, Hattie. All I really need is directions to Mr. Sloan's farm."

"Don't get no visitors up on Hubbard Mountain." Hattie's head snapped up and she pinned Adrienne with her blue eyes. "Kendrick Sloan ain't even got a mailbox. Ain't respectable not to have a box. Even Leander and Dovie do without nowadays. They ask at the post office now and again but they mostly don't get nothin' since their boy, Cabe, passed on. Sloan gets even less. Mighty strange to my way of thinkin'. You some kind of kin?"

"No," Adrienne supplied, losing some of her smile under Hattie's intense gaze. "I'm here on business."

That brought a boisterous laugh. Adrienne didn't know whether or not she'd just been insulted and thought better of asking. "Can you direct me to the Sloan farm, Hattie?"

"I told ya' it cain't hardly be called a farm no more. Boney Martin delivered a truckload of cinder block up there last year. Said it looked to him like Sloan was building a runty lookin' silo, only half as big as the regular kind—which made sense, what with Leander's luck in farmin'. Hired some of the local boys to put the thing up and they came back and said 'tweren't no silo at all but an observatory. You know, a house for one of them telescopes? Cain't figure it, can you? Sloan's got hi'self the highest mountain around and he cain't make out the stars to his likin'."

Fifteen minutes later, Adrienne still hadn't got the information she needed. First she had to hear all about the big shiny tiles Sloan had put on the roof of his house to gather up heat from the sun. Then she had to listen to Hattie's description of the house itself. "Fit for a king, that's fer sure. Three stories high it is, with four chimneys. Got more fireplaces than anybody'd need. Even got a big old balcony like you see on them foreign castles. Used the best stone masons and carpenters around, Sloan did. Went up like lightnin'."

Even if what Hattie told her wasn't what Adrienne wanted to know, it did start her thinking. How could a man whose only income was supposed to be the disability compensation he received from the air force afford to build a private observatory and construct a solar-heated home? Had she arrived too late? Had some other company already discovered Sloan's creative talent and placed him on their payroll?

"Leander works for Mr. Sloan but who does Sloan work for?" Adrienne asked, knowing she was trying to find out something that was really none of her business. "That house must have cost a fortune to build."

As usual, Hattie's answer was much more and much less than the one she was hoping for. "He's got money but no one's saying where it comes from. I got my ideas but it ain't fittin' for me to say. If'n I speak out of turn, I don't rightly know what might happen."

An odd expression crossed her thin, lined face. "Being from the city and all, you probably ain't scared of haints, are ya'?"

"Haints?" Adrienne repeated the unfamiliar word.

"Haints," Hattie said again, a note of reverence in her tone. "Ghostly spirits that commence t'rattlin' their chains and the like. Been a lot of haints up on Hubbard's Mountain in recent days. Some folks say it's Cabe Hubbard who got killed a while ago in a plane crash what's causin' them bright lights in the sky. Could be that brave boy's spirit tryin' to fly his ghostly plane back home to be with his folks."

"You actually believe that?" Adrienne blurted. The unsettling sensation she'd only recently quelled came back to her stomach. Maybe she hadn't been imagining things last night. Maybe she wasn't the only one who'd witnessed a UFO landing.

She realized she was dealing with superstitious people, people who might explain what she'd seen last night as one of these "haints." Had Hattie undergone an experience similar to hers? "You've seen one of these spirits?"

"Naw," Hattie denied indifferently, shrugging her bony shoulders. "I ain't ever seen no haint. All they ever is is somebody scarin' somebody, usually. Still, I can't help but think when Sloan brought Cabe's personals back to his grievin' kin, somethin' got riled. He stayed on, and ever since folks've been talkin' 'bout strange doin's on the mountain. Sometimes I swear I've heard the devil's own music stirrin' in the trees.''

Hattie paused to let that sink in, then continued. "None of us knows where Sloan hails from and we ain't askin'. He's an odd one, that's fer sure. Dovie and Leander just ain't the same folks since Sloan come. I asked Dovie if Sloan would like me to take by a few bottles of my spring elixir and she tol' me he don't abide strangers droppin' in unexpected."

Adrienne was grateful that after her speech, the elderly woman dropped into a thoughtful silence. She wasn't up to hearing much more on the subjects of "haints" or the devil. She'd survived her share of terror last night and she didn't want to think about the possibility of it happening again.

Neither did the local opinion of Kendrick Sloan ease her mind. She had a job to do and was determined to do it but now she had some serious reservations. Maybe Lang Manufacturing shouldn't get involved with a kook, and she was beginning to think Kendrick Sloan might turn out to be just that. On the other hand, her doubts weren't based on personal observation.

After coming this far, it didn't make much sense to go back just because Hattie May Carson had said that Kendrick Sloan was a strange man who didn't like company. Hattie May wasn't exactly the average woman on the street. Adrienne imagined the phone conversation she'd have with Ted Erwin to explain why she hadn't followed through. *Ted, I'm not meeting that Sloan guy. Hattie May Carson told me his mountain might be haunted.* Her boss would laugh himself sick.

Still, the more she heard about Sloan, the more questions she had. She ticked the most nagging ones off in her mind. Why had the man chosen such an unlikely spot to finish recuperating from his accident, and what exactly was his relationship to the Hubbards? What was the source of his income? Did he have something to do with these ghostly displays that seemed to have started at his arrival? Was he deliberately arranging these frightening events to keep people away from his mountain?

A shiver of nervousness danced up Adrienne's spine. If Sloan had gone to such lengths to scare people off his property, what might he do to keep her away? For a man she'd assumed was handicapped by serious injury, a fallen hero from the armed services, he certainly seemed to have earned himself a strange reputation. Billy Lee Carson had out-and-out refused to talk about him, and according to what Hattie May had told her, Sloan was definitely not considered a model member of the community.

Then again, perhaps the poor man had been so scarred or crippled by his serious accident that he couldn't bear to have anyone see him. If Leander and Dovie were good friends or relatives of his, they might very well cater to his need for absolute privacy. Adrienne could certainly understand it if that were the case, but hoped it wouldn't result in her being turned away before she could make her offer.

If she could just talk to him, she knew she could convince Sloan to sign on with Lang. The arrangement would be perfect for a man like him. They could work through the mail. If he were willing to sell his designs, his creative ideas, he wouldn't need to see anyone or leave his mountain hideaway. The man might not like strangers dropping in but she was positive he'd change his attitude once she'd told him why she had come.

By sticking to direct questions, Adrienne was finally able to exact the directions from Hattie and was on the road to Hubbard's Mountain less than an hour later. In distance, Sloan's property was only five miles from Rocky Bottom Hollow, but the road was really a beaten-down track that twisted and turned innumerable times as it ascended the mountain. Adrienne was reminded more than once of her recent drive, and was grateful for the bright morning sunshine that lit her wild surroundings.

From the summit, the view was magnificent. The flat-topped, steep-sided ridge joined other subordinate ridges pointing toward the horizon. Below her, Adrienne could see long, fertile valleys cut by streams and ponds that carved into the rich bottom land. Both sides of the road were splashed with color. Tall rhododendrons, spicewood trees and hardy azaleas dotted the landscape with pink, yellow and white flowers.

The road came to an end in a small clearing where she saw a huge, corrugated metal shed. Before she got out of her car, Adrienne looked around. Tucked into the side of the mountain, overlooking a fast-moving stream, was the house Hattie had described.

A narrow rope footbridge spanned the deep gorge between the house and the clearing. It looked as if the only way to get to the house was to walk over the bridge. Its rickety condition made Adrienne sure it had warned off many a fainthearted visitor. She, however, was made of stronger stuff.

Purse in hand, she placed one foot on the first slat. The bridge swayed and groaned. She grabbed the rough hemp safety rail and kept on walking. Cautiously, she took one step after another, making sure her heels didn't get caught in the spaces between the boards. Every inch of the way she chanted, "You'd better be worth it, mister. You damned well better be worth it."

At the halfway mark, she made the foolish mistake of looking down. With one slip of her foot, she could plummet over the edge and splatter on the jagged rocks and boulders far below. She froze in sudden panic. She squeezed her eyes shut, praying for the bridge to stop swaying and her heart to settle back down in her chest where it belonged.

"Oh God, it's happening again," Adrienne groaned as a strong sense of déjà vu swept over her. She couldn't go forward and she couldn't go back. If she tried to turn around, she'd surely fall over the edge. All she needed now was to look up and see a glowing baked potato descending from the sky.

When she heard the low voice, she almost fainted. "The view's better if you open your eyes."

"No," Adrienne moaned. If she opened her eyes, she knew what she'd see and she wasn't going to go through that horror again. One encounter with a green-skinned monster was enough for a lifetime. If she ignored it, maybe it would go away. It had to be that damned figment of her imagination come back to haunt her.

Maybe there was something in the air around here that disagreed with her. She'd left Minnesota a perfectly sane person. With the exception of her decision to make this trip, she'd operated sensibly in Florida. Yet, after less than twenty-four hours in West Virginia, she'd become a candidate for a straitjacket.

"Well, then, do you plan to stand there all day?"

Something that didn't exist wouldn't try to appeal to her reason, would it? Adrienne opened her eyes and immediately felt ridiculous. Standing at the other end of the bridge was a perfectly normal looking human being. Dressed in a pair of baggy fatigues, a faded olive T-shirt and hiking boots, he was only a man whose expression was both curious and amused. Arms folded across a very broad chest, he grinned at her predicament, his eyes moving slowly up and down her trembling form.

"It's not often a fair damsel attempts to cross my drawbridge," he drawled in a deceptively casual tone. "If I were a knight in shining armor, I'd come to your rescue but alas, chivalry is dead. Mind telling me what you're doing up here?"

"You can't be Kendrick Sloan," Adrienne breathed. This man looked as if he'd never been sick a day in his life. He hadn't moved and she wasn't close enough to see if he were disfigured, but he certainly didn't convey an attitude of abject suffering. Cocksure was the term that came to mind and that wasn't a label that had ever come up when she'd imagined Kendrick Sloan.

"Why not?" he inquired.

"Because he's...he's..." Her voice trailed off. She was embarrassed enough without telling him that, apart from the momentary fear she'd had of his being a green-skinned monster, she'd been expecting a hopelessly disfigured man confined to a wheelchair.

Aware that he was waiting for her to finish her sentence, she jabbered nervously, "You look fine. I mean I expected you to be..." *Oh damn!* If this was Kendrick Sloan, she'd already messed up royally. He'd never want to do business with someone who couldn't form a simple sentence without putting her foot in her mouth.

"You look fine, too, and I wasn't expecting you at all," the man retorted smoothly as he stepped up on the bridge. His considerable weight made the ancient timbers creak ominously and his first step renewed the swaying.

Adrienne dropped her purse and grabbed for the railing with both hands. "Don't move!" she ordered hysterically. "Don't take another step."

"Calm down, Angel," he instructed soothingly. "This old bridge can hold both of us. All you have to do is stay put until I come get you."

Staying put was easy. Calming down was impossible. She clung to the rope while the bridge swayed and shivered with every step he took. When he finally reached her and placed one large, tanned hand over each of hers, she was shaking as badly as the slats under her feet.

Without a word, he pried her fingers free of the hemp and before she knew what was happening she was thrown over a very hard, thickly muscled shoulder. He bent his knees and the downward motion added to her fear. Beyond caring, she clutched frantically at his shirt and buried her head between his shoulder blades.

"It's okay. You're okay," he assured. "I'm just picking up your purse. We'll be off the bridge in a few seconds. You're safe." He talked softly to her all the way across the bridge then took several steps onto solid ground before gently setting her down on her feet.

Adrienne stared at him, a red flush coming up from her neck to color her cheeks as she stammered, "Thank you." Her embarrassment increased when she saw him reaching over his shoulder and rubbing his back. His wince was unmistakably caused by the wounds she'd inflicted when she'd dug her fingernails into his flesh. "I'm sorry if I hurt you."

"I've had worse," he dismissed her concern. "Now that you've left your mark on me, mind telling me what you're doing here?"

The face towering over her was so magnificent, Adrienne was momentarily stunned. Then, seeing the knowing expression on his face and realizing he was aware of her fascination, she strove for a cool tone. "Are you Kendrick Sloan?"

"Yeah, so what do you want?"

Swallowing her annoyance at his surly demand, she stated, "I have a proposition to make you."

I'll just bet you do, Kendrick thought to himself. He couldn't wait to see how she was going to proceed with this "proposition" and he wasn't going to make it easy for her. She must have been able to read the lascivious trend of his thoughts from his expression, for she quickly elaborated. "A business venture that might interest you."

"I'm going up to the house," he said baldly. "You can come if you want." He strode away, leaving it up to her whether or not to follow.

Kendrick ground his teeth against the possessive surge that hit him every time he looked at her. Seeing her on that bridge too frightened to move, he'd felt like a spider who had somehow been lucky enough to trap a tiny golden butterfly in his web. Even knowing that the beautiful butterfly was potentially dangerous, he'd longed to keep her entangled permanently. That longing stunned him.

He realized it would have been more accurate if he'd cast himself as a moth and she a brilliant flame that inexorably drew him. He turned his back on that unpleasant image just as he had on the woman who inspired it.

Adrienne fought down her rising temper. The man wasn't even polite enough to request her name, and her statement about a business venture hadn't fostered even the barest show of curiosity or surprise—just a lustful look that had made her feel cheap. It was almost as if he'd been expecting her, expected to hear a less than businesslike offer.

But that wasn't possible. Aside from her boss and Rosie, no one else knew she was coming. Even if he had been forewarned, why would he think she had more on her mind than business? Obviously, he was conceited enough to assume all women lusted after his muscle-bound body. Adrienne glared after his departing figure for a moment then shrugged off her irritation and trailed behind him. Kendrick Sloan would soon discover she was not interested in toying with his body, but in his body of toys.

With his long-legged stride and swift, easy gait, he appeared to be fully recovered from the accident that had earned him his discharge from the air force. Next to him, she felt like a midget and had difficulty keeping up. He was yards ahead of her by the time she realized she'd have to run to catch him. Speeding across the rough terrain in spike heels would be the height of folly and she'd already played the fool once for him today.

Besides, it was a relief to be out from under the potent force of his probing green eyes. As she leisurely ambled along in his wake, she looked at his departing figure. He was one of the most perfect specimens of manhood that it had ever been her good fortune to meet. He walked with a marvelous coordination, and a sense of timing at each step that made her want to whistle. She wondered what he'd do if she did just that. Macho men rarely liked it when the shoe was on the other foot.

Smiling with that thought, she found herself staring at the play of muscles beneath his T-shirt and pants. Several feet later, she was still trying to assimilate what she'd learned. Kendrick Sloan wasn't handicapped or disfigured. He was tanned, tough and gorgeous!

With his blue-black hair, those incredible eyes with their lush black lashes and his clean-cut features, he'd probably retreated to this remote mountaintop to avoid hordes of predatory women. It was going to be extremely difficult not to become one of the horde. To think she'd actually expected to feel sorry for him. The only one she felt sorry for was herself.

Instead of making a grand entrance and impressing him with her sophistication and business acumen, she'd come across as a wimpy nitwit. At least she hadn't disclosed that her terror was based on more than a fear of heights. He'd really think she was a nut if she admitted that for a few seconds, she'd wondered if he were a silver-coated alien dropping down from the heavens.

For the rest of her time in West Virginia, in her dealings with Kendrick Sloan, she had to put that terrifying incident out of her head. She refused to let one weird nightmare throw her like this. If it hadn't been a dream, then there was a perfectly logical explanation for what had happened. It was unfortunate that she couldn't think of one at the moment, but it would occur to her someday. Meanwhile, she was going to go about her business as if nothing had happened.

In that vein, she looked up and noted that Kendrick Sloan had disappeared into the house. Arriving on the doorstep, she hesitated. Should she just walk in or ring the doorbell? Years of parental lecturing reminded her that one didn't walk into anyone's home uninvited. "You can come if you want" didn't strike her as a real invitation.

While she deliberated, she eyed the imposing structure. Hattie May was right. Any king would be happy to claim the place as a country home. It was like a miniature castle even down to the moatlike stream. Was chivalry really dead? The resident knight lacked manners but he lived in a style Lancelot would have envied.

"Are you waiting for me to carry you over the threshold or do you think you can make it yourself this time?" Kendrick spoke from the screened doorway.

"Speak of the devil," Adrienne muttered under her breath.

"If you're trying to sell me something Angel, I'd watch what you call me."

"My name's not Angel, it's Adrienne Castle," she declared, attempting to regain some lost ground.

Kendrick shouldered open the door, deliberately leaving limited space for her to pass through. "You're welcome in mine anytime, Princess." Challenge sparkled in his green eyes and brought a devilish tilt to his lips.

With a regal toss of her head, Adrienne picked up the challenge. With the haughtiness of a queen, she said, "We would be most pleased, sir."

Chin up, nose in the air, she swept past him, her heart leaping into her throat as her arm brushed the material of his shirt and registered the warm, hard wall of muscle beneath it. He smelled of the outdoors and clean, male sweat. A coil of pleasure constricted her throat, making it difficult to breathe. She couldn't let him see her reaction, however, and marched ahead of him into a spacious atrium.

Adrienne lifted her head in astonishment. From three stories above, sunshine spilled through a huge skylight. The room was magnificent—as magnificent as the man who owned it.

Kendrick came to a halt behind her and stifled a gasp. Her gold hair shone in the sunlight and made her look every bit the angel he had called her. It was hard for him to remember that her wings were tarnished and her musical voice wasn't inspired by heavenly harps.

She had tilted her head up to find the source of the bright light and her profile was flawless. The urge to take her in his arms and drag her upstairs to the loft was almost insurmountable. The prissy business suit she had on only increased his desire. He knew what was under that layer of tailored wool.

Seeing her in the clear light of day, Kendrick had a change of heart. He really wasn't that fond of his solitude and his project had reached the stage where it didn't require every minute of his time. Perhaps with a little encouragement, Ms. Adrienne Castle would accelerate her plans for his seduction. Forewarned was forearmed. He knew what she was after, but maybe he could have her in his bed without giving it to her.

OUT OF THIS WORLD

So far, she'd been put off by his rudeness. He hadn't been playing his cards right at all. If she was going to lead him astray, he had to be more accommodating. He'd better start acting like the starved-for-a-woman man she'd been sent to entice.

"This is beautiful," Adrienne complimented in an awestruck whisper, her dark eyes taking in the cathedral effect of natural wood beams and polished diagonal panels. A twelve-foot weeping fig tree stood in the center of the room, its leaves glossy in the sunlight. Several other varieties of greenery and flowers were displayed in planters scattered across the slate floor. "I've never seen anything like it."

"Neither have I," Kendrick murmured hoarsely, his voice wrapping around her like a velvet cape. The sound caressed her, seduced her, aroused her.

Adrienne turned slowly to face him, compelled by a force she understood, but which still came as a shock. When she saw the way he was looking at her, she started to tremble. She didn't know where she'd gone wrong, when or how this meeting had digressed into an encounter of such intense intimacy. She'd never been more aware of a man or the kind of responses he created in her body.

She could imagine what he saw in her eyes because she saw the same thing in his—desire, hot and strong. He wanted her and by God, she wanted him, too. He was a stranger and the idea was ridiculous but she wanted nothing more than to run the short distance between them and hurl herself into his arms. What kind of man was he that the sound of his voice could inspire such a violent reaction?

Hardly knowing what she was doing, she began retracing her steps. Lips parted, she moved toward him.

It was as if he were communicating with her through a mind link and she were totally attuned to his wishes. He needed her, and like a willing slave, she yearned to obey.

"Who's come callin'?" a female voice warbled from the hallway leading to the back of the house.

Adrienne didn't see the owner of the voice but was witness to Kendrick's reaction. He looked the way she felt—as if someone had just kicked him in the stomach. To her everlasting gratitude, the strange spell had been broken and she was free. She even managed to smile as she turned to face the woman bustling into the room.

"Dovie, this is Ms. Adrienne Castle and she will be joining us for lunch," Kendrick announced, taking hold of Adrienne's elbow.

"But I—" Adrienne began and was immediately cut off.

"You did want to talk to me, didn't you?" Kendrick asked.

"Well yes, but—"

"Glad to meet'cha," Dovie Hubbard said shyly, thrusting out a work-worn hand. Soft gray eyes twinkled with welcome as she smiled at Adrienne. "We don't get many visitors. We'll be proud to have you share a meal with us."

Adrienne clasped the woman's hand and returned the smile. "Thank you. I'm happy to meet you, too." The woman was aptly named. She looked just like a little dove. She had a soft plump breast, gray hair, velvety eyes and a gentle cooing voice.

"You're in for a treat, Ms. Castle," Kendrick added enthusiastically. "Dovie's souse and sausage is on the menu today. She's had leather breeches on the back burner and cabbage in the frying pan all morning. Her biscuits ought to be about ready to come out of the oven, so we'd best wash up."

Dovie dimpled with embarrassment. "He flatters me. I've never seen a man so plumb silly about cracklins. I apologize if they're a mite dry today but we was gettin' low on lard."

That said, the woman scurried back to her kitchen and Adrienne had the chance to question Kendrick before partaking of these culinary delights she'd never heard of. "Leather breeches? Cracklins?"

"Dried green beans and pork rinds," Kendrick explained, chuckling. His well-modulated voice took on the cadence of the hill country. "Just the thing to fatten you up a mite, honey. Round heah, we lap up Dovie's grub. To stay on my good side, I'll 'spect you to do the same."

Four

Kendrick escorted Adrienne through the spacious living room and pointed up to the railed balcony. Before leaving her on her own, he instructed her to go through the first door on the right at the top of the stairs to find the bathroom. As she mounted the steps, she was struck again by the magnificence of his house.

One wall of the living room was of native stone with a raised hearth and fireplace. Pegged hardwood floors gleamed beneath a scattering of hooked Scandinavian rugs. The furniture matched the room—large, masculine and comfortable. How could he afford to live like this?

Gaining the second floor, she passed through what had to be a small guest room. Making note of the sparse, almost utilitarian furnishings, the empty shelves and unmade narrow bed, she saw that one of Hattie's estimations had been right. According to the looks of the room, Kendrick Sloan didn't encourage many guests. After the stark bedroom, the bathroom came as a real surprise.

Like the atrium, it was huge and lit by the sun. Lush green plants were everywhere. The irregular-shaped tub, sunk into the floor and nearly hidden by the surrounding greenery, looked like a secluded pool in the midst of a tropical forest. Orchids bloomed on vines that clung to one rough stone wall. For a moment she'd thought she'd stepped into a small jungle or a beautifully designed greenhouse.

Remembering the near-primitive plumbing awaiting her back at her motel, Adrienne shuddered. Oh, what she wouldn't give for an hour soaking in that beautiful tub. Almost hidden in one corner of the room was a glass-enclosed shower stall. Adrienne doubted it had the weak and inconsistent water pressure of the one at the Royal Pine.

She nearly stripped off her clothing and stepped inside, but a luncheon awaited her somewhere on the first floor. She hadn't come to Hubbard's Mountain to share a meal with Kendrick Sloan but it would have seemed ungracious to refuse. She was going to have to resign herself to the slower pace of this rural environment. Nothing was going according to plan, but she was a resilient person and could go with the flow.

If Kendrick Sloan wanted to talk business over lunch, fine. She washed her hands, splashed a little water on her face and retouched her lipstick. A look in the mirror made her dive back into her purse for the small brush she always carried.

Swinging upside down over a man's shoulder had left her hair in total disarray. It took more than a few strokes to return her fine, shoulder-length hair to good order. Retrieving her suit jacket from the door knob, she decided against putting it back on and folded it over her arm.

Hurrying back through the bedroom, she descended to the first floor. "Follow your nose," had been the directions she'd been given to the kitchen and she discovered she had no trouble. Delectable aromas had her stomach rumbling and her mouth watering long before she stepped into the large, airy kitchen.

What awaited her there was yet another in a series of shocks. Food enough to feed a veritable army steamed in pans on the stove and in dishes on the counter. Kendrick was the only person in the room. Although she wondered who was supposed to eat all the food, she was glad that they would be alone at the table. They could get right down to business.

Kendrick had changed into a fresh, short-sleeved oxford shirt of pale blue. The black hair around his tanned face was damp and curling from a recent wash. The well-worn fatigues remained, but with his looks and physique, Adrienne thought, he could have posed for the cover of *Gentleman's Quarterly* and set a new fashion trend.

"Dovie had to leave. She packed up a basket and is joining her husband for a picnic lunch in one of the fields," Kendrick explained, picking up a plate and handing it to Adrienne. "Load up."

Adrienne looked skeptically at the array of food. Tentatively, she reached for one of the serving spoons. She had to admit that whatever was cooking smelled much better than it sounded.

"Cracklins," Kendrick supplied, and quickly heaped a portion onto her plate. Before she knew it, the dish was laden with all sorts of things.

With the exception of the sausage and green beans, she could only guess at the composition of the dishes. Everything looked delicious so she decided not to inquire about the ingredients. In this instance, ignorance might definitely be bliss.

Putting his own heaping plate on the table, Kendrick gallantly pulled out one of the cane chairs for Adrienne. "Best seat in the house," he announced with a sparkling grin. At second look, she decided the grin was a definite smirk.

Though half-convinced she was about to become the victim of a practical joke, Adrienne set her plate down and lowered herself onto the chair. She was prepared to prove to him that she could be a good sport. She would show him she wasn't normally that spineless jellyfish he'd found clinging in white-knuckled terror to the railing of his bridge. Adrienne Marie Castle could handle anything... well almost anything.

Kendrick pushed in her chair, gave her shoulders a squeeze and then bent his head down to hers. His lips at her ear, he whispered, "Eat up or you'll suffer dire consequences."

Without thinking, Adrienne turned her head to deliver a suitable rejoinder but her lips brushed against his chin. She jerked backward, hoping he understood the contact was an accident, not an attempt at a kiss. Trying to act as if nothing had happened, she quipped, "You mean if I don't eat I won't stay on your good side?"

Their faces were just inches apart. Adrienne's eyes widened as she felt the sudden rise of goose bumps on her skin. Inexplicably, she was cold and for one brief second felt a surge of absolute terror. Just as quickly, the feeling disappeared along with the chill. She blinked and as if she'd just returned from another dimension, she was warm again, held spellbound by the heated gaze of a very attractive man.

Straightening, Kendrick drawled, "I'm sure you'll be able to think of a few ways to stay on my good side."

He sauntered over to his own place and sat down before saying, "Actually, I figure you'd better get a lot of fuel in that tiny little body of yours if you intend proposing some sort of business venture to me. I warn you, I'm not easily persuaded by the hard sell tactics of door-to-door saleswomen."

"But you've never come up against someone like me, Mr. Sloan," Adrienne started cheekily, thinking now was as good a time as any to begin talking about Lang's interest in his toys. "I think we—"

"Kendrick, please," he interrupted. "Seems silly to be so formal when we're sitting in my kitchen eating lunch together, don't you agree?"

"All right, and please call me Adrienne," she asked, smiling widely, delighted when he smiled back at her. He had a winning smile. He had a winning everything.

For a long moment, they stared at each other across the table until finally Kendrick cleared his throat and said, "Better start eating or Dovie'll be back here and scold both of us for not cleaning our plates."

Adrienne picked up her fork. "I can't imagine that sweet lady scolding anyone."

Kendrick finished chewing a mouthful of food before commenting, "You'd be surprised what that sweet lady is capable of. She's not quite as soft as she looks. She can bully the best of us."

"You, you mean?" Adrienne teased with a puckish grin.

Pushing a napkin-draped basket toward her, Kendrick admitted, "Me and anyone else she thinks needs it." Staring pointedly at Adrienne's untouched plate, he warned, "Just being a pint-sized beauty won't keep you safe. Clean your plate."

Adrienne had received more than her share of compliments in her life, often in far more florid terms. However, she hadn't expected any from him. He'd made it clear from the outset that he was skeptical of her. Delivered so offhandedly, the compliment seemed sincere and was apparently offered with no ulterior motive in mind. If he kept on saying such things, she'd lose track of the reason for her visit.

She shoved her fork into the "leather breeches" and was delighted with the taste of the bacon-seasoned vegetable. The dried-in-the-pod green beans had evidently been soaked then prepared so expertly that they tasted nearly as fresh as the day they'd left the vine.

Experimentally, she tasted each item on her plate and was soon making a sizable dent in the mountain of food. The cracklins were crisp and flavorful, like a snack food she could easily become addicted to. The sausage was the best she'd ever had. The cabbage, allegedly fried all morning, was delicately flavored with herbs and had been lightly sautéed in a meaty broth. She popped a forkful of the jellied pork tidbits into her mouth.

"Souse is an acquired taste," Kendrick commented with a knowing grin, eyeing the startled expression on her face when the pickled concoction hit her taste buds. "I won't even tell you what parts of the pig go into it."

Swallowing with a gulp, Adrienne reached for her water glass in an attempt to rinse the sharp flavor from her tongue. "You might have warned me," she accused.

"And miss the look on your face?" he defended, his grin softening the compelling intensity of his verdant eyes.

The meal continued comfortably, each teasing the other as though they'd known each other for years instead of minutes. While Adrienne was thoroughly enjoying herself, it seemed strange to her that Kendrick hadn't yet demanded to know exactly what business she was in. Eventually, she told him. "I'm a representative of Lang Manufacturing. Wouldn't you like to know why I've come to see you?"

He didn't answer immediately but his expression sobered and he seemed to be looking past her when he finally said, "I think we should enjoy this pleasant time together and put off talking business for a while longer."

She frowned at the wistful note in his tone. "What I'm about to propose to you won't be so unpleasant," she said, wanting to assure him that she had only his best interests in mind. "This could be your lucky day, Kendrick."

"I don't believe in luck, Adrienne," he returned swiftly, the sparkle dying out of his eyes.

Taken aback by the sober comment, Adrienne was equally unnerved by the sudden attention he paid to her. His eyes traveled with infinite slowness from the top of her shining head and down her face. They lingered at the tiny pulse that throbbed at her throat then swept lower to the full curve of her breasts beneath her pale pink blouse. She quickly lowered her face, pretending total concentration on her plate.

For some reason, Kendrick felt betrayed by the woman seated across from him. Until she'd reminded him of her reason for coming, he'd almost forgotten that she wasn't interested in him but in his invention. She was a devious, diminutive Delilah, willing to use her body to garner his secrets.

The lace trim of her slip showed faintly through the silky fabric of her blouse, a reminder of what a very feminine enchantress she was. It would take some doing to remain immune. He wondered if she knew how susceptible he could be to her brand of persuasion.

For a few minutes, he'd wanted to apologize for scaring her last night but she didn't deserve an apology. Evidently, Trenton operated on a need-to-know basis and hadn't told her what kind of invention they were after or she wouldn't have misjudged what she'd seen. Her fear then hadn't been an act, but that didn't mean she wasn't acting now. She might look like a harmless pixie but he knew otherwise. Thank God Gwinnett had made the connection between her and Trenton. If not, Kendrick knew he'd already be a goner.

"This is strictly on the level," Adrienne insisted after a few moments. "I didn't come halfway across the country on a lucky guess. I know my business and I'm willing to pay generously for what I want. If you'll just give me a chance to tell you what my company is offering, I promise you won't be sorry."

"Won't I?" Kendrick scraped back his chair and stood up. "You'll have to forgive me for breaking this up, Adrienne, but I have several things I've got to do this afternoon.''

Adrienne had never been subjected to such an obvious and impolite brush-off. At first, she strangled on a tide of indignation but then she took herself in hand. It wasn't as though she hadn't been forewarned. Her luncheon companion had obviously lapsed temporarily into good manners, and had just now reverted to form.

''No problem,'' she stated calmly. Getting up, she allowed herself to be ushered out of the kitchen but stopped before they reached the front door. ''I know I arrived unannounced. Would you have time to talk to me this evening over dinner?''

The look he gave her didn't foster much hope for a positive response so his next words were a surprise. ''Perhaps I could make time.''

''It'll be at my expense,'' she encouraged.

''That's a matter of opinion but I take it you mean you'll be paying the check.''

Ignoring his sarcasm she continued brightly, ''Would seven o'clock be convenient?'' At his nod of agreement, she went on, ''I'll pick you up and let you name the place. I'm staying at the Royal Pine but I'm still unfamiliar with the area.''

''No, I'll pick you up,'' he negated. ''Be ready at seven.'' He gave her a last piece of advice as he ushered her firmly out the door. ''If you want to avoid the moat, go around to the back door of the house and follow the driveway down to the clearing.''

Hand raised and poised to knock, Kendrick caught his breath when the door swung open and Adrienne stood before him.

"Hello," she greeted with a smile. "You're right on time."

At least he had the presence of mind to return her smile but could only mumble a response. He waited at the door, enjoying the view. The soft peach fabric of her dress swirled around her legs with each step. The rustling sound it made as she moved called out in provocative invitation. He breathed deeply of the scent filling the sparse cabin, transforming the rude shelter into a bower of flowers.

"That's some dress," he complimented, his voice constricted.

Hastily, Adrienne draped a cashmere stole carefully around her shoulders and across her bosom, wishing she were throwing it over a shapeless, high-necked, long-sleeved granny gown. "Thank you," she managed awkwardly.

What had possessed her to wear this voile, spaghetti-strapped dress? This was supposed to be a business dinner and she'd donned the most flattering, revealing and ultrafeminine garment she had brought with her. His eyes hadn't moved from her chest since she'd opened the door.

"You remind me of the spring blossoms that grow up on my mountain." Sniffing the air, he declared brusquely, "Smell like one, too."

No doubt about it, she should have left on her navy suit. Not only would it have set the proper tone for the evening, but it would have done a far better job hiding her body's instant response to the soft-spoken compliments. The sound of his voice wasn't the only thing that was playing havoc with her senses. The sight of him in the open doorway was enough to incite every erogenous zone in her body. She knew without looking that her nipples were pointedly apparent beneath her bodice.

That morning, she'd thought he was probably the sexiest man alive and he'd been wearing a pair of tattered fatigues and an old T-shirt. This evening, his appeal was even greater. In a pale blue sportscoat, gray slacks and a creamy, open-necked shirt, he was lucky she didn't tell him she'd like to forego dinner and dine on his delicious body. It was going to be awfully hard to keep her mind on patents, residuals and marketing strategy.

Her goal for the evening was to convince him of the seriousness of her offer to buy all rights to that little spaceship and any new designs he'd come up with. How could he take her seriously in a dress fit for a romantic dinner for two? It probably wouldn't do any good to explain that she'd been on vacation and didn't have anything else to wear. It would only sound like a lie since he'd already seen the navy suit.

Chin up, Adrienne, she instructed. It's the kind of deal you're proposing that's important, not what you're wearing. Besides, the suit hadn't impressed him with her seriousness and business acumen earlier, maybe femininity would now. "Ready when you are," she remarked with false gaiety and started for the door.

I'm ready to throw you on that bed, Kendrick wanted to shout but instead merely stepped aside and allowed her to pass through the doorway in front of him. "My car's right over there," he said, taking her elbow and guiding her down the gravel walkway toward a large silver sedan.

They exchanged inane pleasantries about the weather and the flowers blooming alongside the path while Kendrick fought the urge to turn Adrienne around and march her right back into her cabin. As far as he was concerned, they could forget all about dinner. Another stronger hunger superseded his body's need for food.

He nearly groaned aloud when he helped her into the car and her wrap slipped off one bare shoulder, affording him a nice view of shadowed cleavage and ripe curves. What little there was at the top of her dress was held up by two minuscule straps that tied at the shoulder. Fleetingly, his fingers tingled with temptation. How easy it would be to undo those fragile supports, release those luscious breasts he'd freed the night before.

This time, he knew he wouldn't hold back his urges and remain impersonal in his touch. And this time, he wouldn't want her unconscious. He'd want to watch her soft eyes grow dark with desire, watch her creamy skin flush with excitement, hear her cries for fulfillment when he turned his fantasies of her into reality.

And Adrienne? Abruptly his desire was replaced by rage. Oh, she'd want to be fully awake, he was sure. No matter how repugnant she might find his body, she'd never show it. She'd been sent to extract every bit of information possible from him, to try to convince him to go with Trenton instead of Aerospace. What better time to further her cause than when he was so desperate for her, he'd tell her anything to get her into bed?

Wasn't that where this farcical evening was leading? He knew it was. If he'd doubted her duplicity earlier, the sexy dress had given her away. There was nothing businesslike about the utter lack of fabric covering her smooth back or the way the scrap of her bodice revealed her breasts. That is, unless her business was the oldest profession in the world.

He'd be a fool to turn down the bargain she was willing to offer, but he cursed her motivation, and himself for not having better resistance. The obscenity of this subterfuge seemed all the greater because it was being perpetrated by one so young, so seemingly soft and untouched, so innocently alluring.

Damn you, Trenton, he cursed as he stalked around the car and got in. Throwing it in gear, he pressed down hard on the accelerator. Rocky Bottom Hollow was left behind in seconds.

Alarmed by their speed and a little bit frightened by the glowering expression on Kendrick's face, Adrienne slammed her feet on imaginary brakes and took a firm grip on the armrest. "In a hurry to eat?" she asked, hoping her light, teasing tone hid her unease.

"In a hurry to get this over," he growled.

It had happened again. One minute she was dealing with Mr. Nice Guy and the next, a scowling Darth Vader. The man had more moods than chameleons had colors. Unfortunately, most of them were dark and unattractive.

"What's the matter?" she asked, dismayed.

"Sorry," Kendrick responded, slowing the vehicle but not softening the firm set of his jaw. "Forget I said that."

His granite jaw discouraged further conversation. He kept his eyes directed ahead and Adrienne supposed she should be grateful for his inattention to her, for the road was winding and treacherous. He offered no explanation for his fast takeoff or his surliness and Adrienne decided it would be wisest not to demand one. Instead, she relaxed back into the butter-soft upholstery of the luxurious car. At least she no longer had to fear he'd lose control of the vehicle and hurtle them over the edge of the road and down the mountainside.

Nevertheless, after another glance at the hardened features of the man seated beside her, sensing the power in his hands as he expertly controlled the car through a series of wicked turns, Adrienne wondered if she might survive an automobile accident more easily than Kendrick's wrath. She could almost see the black cloud hovering over his head and she didn't want to be an innocent victim of a sudden cloudburst.

Going over every detail of the last few minutes, and the time they'd spent together during lunch, she could think of no reason he should be angry with her. If anyone had a right to be angry, she did! "Look here, Mr. Sloan, I don't know what's got your back up, but I'd like to get it out in the open."

"We've reverted to formality, have we?"

"From your attitude, I assumed you'd prefer it."

"You wouldn't like to hear what I'd prefer to call you," he drawled dangerously.

Adrienne swiveled in her seat. She could not figure this man out, but whatever his problem, she'd had enough. After all, he was the one who had the most to gain from their future association. Once she'd gotten his name on a contract, her job would be done. She'd be out scouting new products but he could sit back and enjoy his profits. "What is it with you? Do you always look a gift horse in the mouth or is it just me?"

"Whatever do you mean?" he asked, but his expression was about as innocent as the wolf in grandma's bed.

"You know perfectly well what I'm talking about," Adrienne snapped. "Let's be honest about it. For some reason, I rub you the wrong way and I don't even know how I do it."

Kendrick barked with laughter. She was either innocent or that good an actress. It was about time he found out.

"I'm all for honesty," he began, tossing a sly smile her way. "Let's say I'm disappointed. You want to discuss business and I want to conduct business."

"Conduct it? You don't even know what kind of business I'm in." Adrienne folded her arms over her chest. At last, she was going to be given the opportunity to open the subject she'd been trying to introduce all day. "I thought over dinner I'd be able to make you an offer for your designs. Why does the thought of that discussion make you angry?"

"Because the only designs I have are on your body," he shot back boldly.

"What!"

Enjoying her shock, he increased it. "I want to make love to you, Adrienne Castle. Here, now, in every way I can think of. If we weren't in this car, that's exactly what we'd be doing."

Adrienne was speechless. Her brain ceased to function but her skin reacted by turning crimson. She stared at him as if he'd lost his mind and her expression brought about another rumbling male laugh.

"Don't look so shocked. It's what we both want. I've seen how you look at me and I'm angry because you're postponing the inevitable with all this discussion nonsense."

Even though Adrienne's heart felt as if it had come to a complete stop, she found she could still speak.

"Who do you think you are, God's gift to women? Well, I've got news for you, buddy, you're not!"

"You said you wanted honesty, Adrienne. I'm offering myself to you on a silver platter. Isn't that what you've been after all along?"

Adrienne almost choked. This man wasn't a kook. He was an egomaniac. Lang didn't need Sloan's designs this badly. There were other designers and other toymakers who would jump at the chance to have their creations mass-produced.

"If I'd known you were so deeply involved in a love affair with yourself, I wouldn't have bothered coming to this godforsaken place," she declared nastily. "After this disgusting demonstration, I can *honestly* say we no longer have anything to discuss. Now turn this car around. This meeting is over!"

She breathed a hearty sigh of relief when he immediately complied with her wishes. At the next curve, he executed a sharp U-turn and the car sped along in the opposite direction. She fumed in her seat. The man might be a creative genius but as a human being he was a total washout. She'd just have to tell Ted that since Lang didn't manufacture mirrors, it didn't have anything worthwhile to offer Kendrick Sloan.

They had traveled less than a mile when Kendrick turned off the highway and onto a dirt road. Before Adrienne's protest could leave her mouth, he had stopped the car and switched off the ignition. "What do you think you're doing?" she squeaked as he reached for her.

"Don't be afraid, Angel," Kendrick soothed in a velvety tone, but his grasp was firm as he pulled her across the seat and onto his lap. "If this is goodbye, I have to kiss you. I'm sorry this is the end instead of the beginning but as they say, half a loaf is better than none.''

''Let go of me, you—''

The hand cradling her jaw closed the rest of her sentence and the heated lips that pressed against hers made her forget what she was trying to say. The arm wrapped around her waist was possessive and strong, yet made no attempt to bruise. The kiss ended nothing and started too much.

Adrienne was mystified by her instantaneous reaction. Each thrust of his tongue between her lips was like the injection of a potent aphrodisiac. She wanted to resist but was swiftly overcome by a heavy overdose of desire. He claimed her will by deliberate seduction, his mouth drawing sweetly, his tongue delving deeper and deeper.

When he finally lifted his lips away to nuzzle her throat, her ear, the back of her neck, she was in a euphoric daze, her own lips wantonly seeking the taste of his skin. Her fingers plowed through the thick mane of his hair and held his head secure. She kissed his temple, his cheek, then parted her lips, anticipating the return of his tormenting mouth over hers.

She gasped as he shifted her in his lap and she felt the strength of his arousal beneath her thighs. Instead of taking her offered lips, he bent her backward over one arm, then used his free hand to pull on the fragile ties at her shoulders. Inserting one finger in the bodice of her dress, he dragged it down to her waist, then feasted his eyes. With careful attention to detail, he studied her, his expression rapt.

''What a lovely color you are,'' he murmured. ''Not a wildflower on my mountain has the delicate pink of your breasts.''

Adrienne melted inside at the words, knowing she should be embarrassed, but oddly, she was not. She loved the admiration in his eyes, wanted him to touch her. She couldn't seem to do anything but sigh with pleasure as he cupped one breast, testing its weight in his palm. His eyes glowed with desire as he flicked gently at the nipple with his thumb and it withdrew into a tiny rosebud.

Kendrick smiled at her soft moan and his fingers immediately began stroking her creamy flesh. Perhaps he couldn't have her completely but she'd never forget him. Then again, maybe he could persuade her to make love even if she had nothing to gain but the pleasure of it.

"And no flower petal could be as soft and silky as this," he said hoarsely, then lowered his head so his lips could enjoy the same gratification as his fingers and palm. "So sweet," he groaned just before he enveloped the nipple in his mouth and suckled.

A shiver of excitement, acute pleasure and shock shot up Adrienne's spine. She arched her back as if in further invitation but in truth, the keen bolt of feeling had instantly sobered her. She was painfully aware that it was much, much too late to convince him that she didn't want him, didn't like his kisses and caresses.

She was frightened, badly frightened by her own need. He was a stranger yet he was the only man who had ever inspired such a tempest of wanting within her. Before she was totally lost in the maelstrom, she had to stop him.

"No, Kendrick...please," she begged, pulling back from the sweet trap of his mouth. "You have to stop."

Although it took him by surprise, Kendrick could feel the desperation in her. It was almost as if she were scared. Had she suddenly recognized him as the creature who had tended to her last night? Had she really believed that was what she'd seen? If so, he could explain. It would be a damned sight more convenient and better for all concerned if he never had to, but if she was truly that terrified, he'd have to tell her what she'd really witnessed.

Reluctantly, he straightened away from her and drew up the bodice to cover her tender breasts. "Is it still goodbye, Adrienne?" he asked, dreading her answer.

Adrienne's fingers were shaking as she fumbled with the ties of her dress and one was still undone as she slid off Kendrick's lap. Once safely on the other side of the car, she managed to secure the second tie but her trembling didn't cease. "I don't understand how I could have . . . I've never—"

"Couldn't you convince yourself it's worth it this time?" Kendrick asked, very much afraid he was about to resort to begging. He ached with wanting her. Good or bad, she was the only one who could put him out of his misery. "I know you want my designs but couldn't you settle for me instead?"

He raked a hand through his hair, angry with himself for being unable to fend off his raging desire. "Damn you, Adrienne. Isn't what we just shared worth more to you than your cut? Are you that greedy? If you are, maybe I can . . ."

Disgust for her and himself rose like bile in his throat but a stronger sensation refused to abate. His celibacy had gone on too long and now he was out of control. All he could think about was having her in his bed, sinking into her softness, losing himself within her.

The bitter tone of his voice conveyed the inner battle he had waged and lost. "I can't give you the contract but I could still make it worth your while."

"Are you saying . . . ? Did you think I came here to seduce you into signing a contract with us?" Adrienne couldn't understand how he could have reached such an off-base conclusion. Had some other company attempted such a thing? Had they been successful?

She didn't even want to think about that possibility and not only because she found such tactics revolting. She knew those kinds of things happened but neither she nor Lang Manufacturing did business that way. On the verge of tears from all the emotions she'd had to endure in the space of one short hour, her voice sounded shaky as she said, "I'm sorry, Kendrick. Your toy spaceship and those action figures are pretty special, but all I intended to offer for them was some good old-fashioned American dollars, not my body."

Every word she uttered helped to salvage her bruised pride. "Let me also say that I've never been so insulted. I have no intention of going to bed with you but if I did, it wouldn't be for money. Actually, I feel sorry for you. You may be the best-looking man I've ever seen but since you've stooped to making such a low offer, you've lost all your appeal."

Judging by his behavior earlier on, Adrienne expected an angry outburst to follow that statement. She was shocked when Kendrick looked as if he'd just been poleaxed. Maybe she was the one who'd made a wrong assumption but it certainly sounded as if he'd been berating her for trying to sell herself to him.

Perhaps he was stunned that she no longer found him attractive and had turned down his offer.

Evidently, Kendrick Sloan had never met a woman that wouldn't trade her integrity for a turn in his bed. Oh, she had responded to his incredible looks but at least she'd had the good sense to call a halt before completely compromising herself. Talk about casting pearls before swine. "I'd like to go back to the Royal Pine now," she ordered, her voice as cold as her gaze.

"Good God!" Kendrick placed both hands on the steering wheel, his knuckles white as he ground out between clenched teeth, "I don't think you're lying."

Five

――――

Lying? Any other sins you'd care to lay at my doorstep before never darkening it again?'' Adrienne's brown eyes flashed as she considered whether or not to get out of the car and start walking back to Rocky Bottom Hollow.

The decision was made as soon as she remembered what kind of creatures lurked in the night. If she didn't want to risk that again, she had no choice but to stick it out with this jerk until he took her back to her motel. She tried to speed up the process. ''Can we go now, please.''

''I don't think so.'' Kendrick seem preoccupied but his tone was firm.

''I can't understand why a nice guy like Greg Robinson considers you such a good friend,'' Adrienne flung out in frustration.

That produced a very noticeable wince and a shaken sigh. "Greg? That's how you found out about the toys? He's the one who told you?"

Having made up her mind that Lang Manufacturing had a sound future without the creative endeavors of one Kendrick Sloan, Adrienne had nothing to lose by her sarcasm. "I hate to break this to you, Kendrick, but your creative talent hasn't been announced on the national news. Your namesake happens to be my nephew's best friend."

Swiftly and cuttingly she explained how she'd learned about his craftsmanship and ended with, "I'm no Mata Hari for God's sake. We're talking about a toy spaceship here, not a matter of national defense."

As soon as the words were out of her mouth, she had a very startling thought. What if... What if Kenny's spaceship had served as a model for the real thing? Part of the nation's defense system? No, that was crazy. Last night she'd suffered from her overactive imagination and she wasn't about to allow it to go wild again.

"If you don't want to share your playthings with the rest of the world it's fine by me. There are plenty of other toymakers out there who'd be happy to have their creations marketed by Lang Manufacturing."

Surprisingly, Kendrick agreed, "I'm sure there are."

"So?"

"I don't know what to say, Adrienne."

Kendrick's tone was almost meek and apology was written all over his face. If Adrienne hadn't felt so insulted, and a fool for responding to him like a sex-starved idiot, she might have let him off the hook for misjudging her so badly. There was something in him that had called out to her from the first and still did.

When she looked into those magnificent green eyes of his, why did she see such loneliness and vulnerability? This man was completely self-sufficient. He was impervious to those kinds of feelings. He didn't need the approval of others to feel good about himself.

"I was sent here for one reason only—to propose we put you on retainer," she said indignantly, needing to break the strained silence between them. "Lang wanted to market those toys Kenny showed me and get an option on any others you might have now or create in the future. It appears the last company that approached you was prepared to offer more than money. I hope you're convinced that wasn't what I had in mind."

"I behaved like an ass," Kendrick conceded. "I've completely misjudged you and the situation."

"Yes, you have. Now I'd like to go back to my motel."

"I was wrong about you," Kendrick tried, wishing for some way to break through the barrier she'd erected. "But that doesn't mean we can't take up where... I mean I'd like to show you that I'm not a complete jerk."

"That won't be necessary, Mr. Sloan," she returned frigidly, hoping her dismissive tone would get through his fat head. If he thought she'd ever be willing to take up where they'd left off he was out of his mind. She had her pride.

"Oh, hell. Have it your own way," he bit out in frustration and started up the car.

They rode in silence for at least a mile, Adrienne crowding the passenger door and Kendrick punishing the gas pedal. "And I would like to get back in one

piece," she snapped when he took a dangerous down-
hill curve at breakneck speed.

"Sorry," he grunted and slowed down to a pace that
would have made a snail proud.

If this newest tactic was meant to get a rise out of
her, it would fail, Adrienne decided. His childishness
only served to add more credence to her conclusion
that he wasn't right for Lang. She'd come on a wild-
goose chase all right, and found herself a real turkey!
She would treat these next few minutes as just pen-
ance for her impetuosity.

"Okay!" Kendrick exploded, making Adrienne
jump. "I treated you like a tramp but it was only because I thought you were after..." He floundered for
several seconds then concluded vaguely, "Something
else."

"I know what you thought I was after but believe
me, your toys are the only things you've got that I was
interested in. Note the 'was', Mr. Sloan. It might give
you a hint where our business now stands."

Adrienne had to hold on for dear life as once again
the car took off like a rocket. She dared one glance at
her driver and didn't like what she saw. Kendrick's
features were contorted with anger. He looked as if he
were the injured party. She was the one who'd ended
up stripped to the waist only to discover that the man
kissing her bare breasts considered her a body for hire.
It was humiliating! Degrading!

Also, it didn't make a whole lot of sense. Replaying
everything in her mind, she had to admit that Kendrick hadn't really done anything she hadn't wanted
him to do, and she had loved every minute of it. He'd
been tender, warm, extremely passionate—true, but it
hadn't been anything but lust. Since that was all there

was between them, what other suspicions did he have about her? What could have caused the agony in his voice when he'd finally made the offer to pay for her services?

I thought you were after something else. His words came back to her followed by an image of the odd look on his face when she'd made the statement that Kenny's saucer was only a toy. Could her crazy idea have been close to the truth? Another even more unsettling image came to mind. A silver-wrapped creature descending from the sky. How close to Hubbard's Mountain had she been last night?

No, if she had wandered in on some top secret government test, she would've been immediately surrounded by the military and taken into custody. Yet hadn't Phyllis Robinson told her that while Kendrick had still been a pararescueman, he'd submitted several ideas to enhance the proficiency and safety of his crew? Hadn't she also said that he'd been creating futuristic things for years? What if one of his designs had found a home with NASA?

Putting that together with his interest in astronomy, the strange reputation he had with the people in town, and his preference for living in almost total isolation, Adrienne was almost positive she was on the right track. Kendrick's early retirement could have been just a ruse to cover his involvement in the space program. She'd seen no evidence of the horrendous accident he'd supposedly been in. That story might be what the government wanted the world to believe, so no one would question his sudden departure from the service.

If Kendrick was designing a better spacecraft or some such thing, it could explain what she'd seen the night before. That was it! She hadn't had a close encounter at all! The man in the silver spacesuit hadn't been some alien vegetable creature but an astronaut or a scientist conducting a test of some kind. Had Kendrick been the mastermind behind the decision to scare her out of her wits?

Of course! That was why she hadn't been detained. Her fear had been so obvious, they'd thought it more provident to let her go on thinking she'd just witnessed an alien visitation. Who would ever believe her if she went around trying to convince people of that? She'd be judged a crackpot and the security of their project would remain intact.

It was all so simple, so logical. She could kick herself for not realizing it before. She'd often speculated that the government was behind these strange incidents of UFO sightings and she'd been right. Her family had always laughed at her contention that scientists were at work in secret locations all over the country and that one of them could have already created a spacecraft with far more capabilities than those the public was aware of. Well, she was going to have the last laugh.

It was much more than possible that Kendrick Sloan was a NASA scientist. Langley Research Center, a prime site for aeronautic research, was in West Virginia. It wasn't all that far away. Maybe he was connected with them or Goddard Space Flight in Maryland. She was up on this kind of thing and was familiar with all NASA's field centers. Wallops Island Flight Center, for example, was in Virginia, too. It provided tracking services and launched small orbital missions. Kendrick's observatory might be tied in with the work going on there.

Or he could be associated with one of the hundreds of private industries involved in space research. His house was expensive, far beyond the means of a retired air force technical sergeant. Maybe it was actually owned by either the government or some corporation as a cover for a research installation. She hadn't seen all of it. It wouldn't surprise her if the rest was filled with whirring, beeping computers and research equipment.

It was all beginning to make sense. She might even find it excusable, except for the liberties that had been taken with her mind and her body. She was a United States citizen and had rights! She wasn't sure which one of them they had violated but surely her mistreatment was covered under the Bill of Rights.

She knew it hadn't been Kendrick who'd partially stripped her and kissed her. One of his henchmen had very weird eyes; she'd have to be on the lookout for him. She only hoped she hadn't been exposed to legions of probing eyes. Regardless of who or how many had been in on the peep show, she felt exposed, soiled. She clutched her shawl more tightly over her bosom.

If Kendrick had been directly involved in last night's subterfuge, it must have been quite a shock for him to find her on his doorstep this morning. No wonder he hadn't wanted to discuss anything to do with his designs. He must have assumed that his fear tactic hadn't worked. He probably had thought she was a tough, seasoned spy, able to surmount such adversity.

Considering all she'd endured during the past twenty-four hours, Adrienne had a sudden perverse wish to start speaking in fluent Russian. Luckily, she had enough sense to realize that would only get her more deeply involved. Under the circumstances, she wanted the option of getting out while the getting was good. But Kendrick Sloan hadn't seen the last of her, that was for sure.

He didn't know it, but the man had enough to fear from her without her being a foreign agent. Neither Kendrick Sloan nor anyone else had the authority to put her through the kind of terror and personal humiliation she'd experienced without explanation or apology. They were just lucky she hadn't needed to be carted away to the funny farm.

She was a patriot. She could be trusted. She'd never divulge government secrets.

However, now that she knew what was going on, her curiosity was eating her alive. Her love for science fiction had developed along with an intense desire to become the first female astronaut. The whole universe was out there just waiting for mankind and she had always yearned to be one of the explorers.

Unfortunately, she'd had to accept that she'd never reach an altitude beyond the range of a commercial airliner. Astronaut training took years beyond the time involved obtaining a degree in science or engineering, and acquiring professional experience. In addition, one had to be in top physical condition and be able to endure heat, cold, weightlessness, long periods of time in tight quarters and many other tests of survival. As much as she might have wanted to be an astronaut, she'd been forced to admit that she liked her creature comforts more. There had also been the results of aptitude tests and class scores that reduced her chance of a career in science.

Until tonight, her dreams of adventure had been reluctantly relegated to the past. Though she admired Sally Ride and the other women in the space program, she hadn't wanted to trade places with them. She'd used her vivid imagination to foster her career in marketing and those times when she'd needed an additional outlet for her fantasies, she'd taken in a science fiction movie.

Now, however, if she played her cards right, a golden opportunity was here. She'd yearned for adventure all of her life and the man who could give it to her was seated not three feet away. Beyond that, she was going to find visible proof that she hadn't been seeing things last night. No one but her would ever see that proof, but it would do wonders for her peace of mind.

"Perhaps I'm being unfair to you, Kendrick," she said softly, gratified as he immediately reduced speed and gave her his attention. "I've been thinking it over and I guess I can understand why you were so suspicious. You did apologize but I was too upset to listen. Now that I've calmed down, I think we should talk."

She gave him her sweetest all-is-forgiven smile. "If you're still willing to let me take you to dinner, I'd like to tell you some more about my company. We really are interested in your marvelous toys."

"That sounds like a reasonable offer," Kendrick acknowledged when Adrienne finished outlining the terms Lang Manufacturing was proposing. "I'd like some time to think about it, though. How long are you planning to stay in West Virginia?" Kendrick asked as their dessert was served.

"As long as it takes to get your name on the dotted line," Adrienne said facetiously. "I can come out tomorrow, see your designs and discuss the contract in more detail. I should think that we could strike a reasonable agreement then. Don't you agree?''

"Not necessarily. Some of my best designs are still in my head. It'll take me a while to get them down on paper for you,'' Kendrick hedged as he dug into his strawberry torte. Tanner Gwinnett would have his head if he let her go before Aerospace was convinced that she was harmless.

He had to stall, keep her in West Virginia, preferably where he could keep an eye on her at all times. He had to figure out a way to get her to accept an invitation to stay at his house. After the way he'd come on to her in the car, that wasn't going to be easy.

He wanted—needed—her close by, and not for reasons of security alone. She had surprisingly long legs and full breasts for a woman so tiny. Just thinking about her body made him ache. But having her in his bed was only one of the reasons he wanted to install her under his roof.

She was so soft and innocent looking. Those huge brown eyes of hers were so trusting, so gentle. Her laughter was contagious. Her smiles came easily, as if she'd never really suffered either physically or mentally. She seemed the essence of all that was good and happy in the world. When he was with her, he could forget all the friends he'd lost, the love he'd missed and the harshness he had endured.

Her physical size might be small but she was no lightweight in the intelligence department. The woman who had just presented a very logical and well thought out business proposal to him bore little resemblance to the frightened woman of the evening before—or to the quivering mass of terror clinging white-knuckled to the bridge railing that day. On those meetings, she'd obviously let her imagination run away with her, but tonight she was the quintessential professional with her feet firmly planted in reality.

Adrienne Castle knew her business and Kendrick was willing to bet all he had that she was very successful at it. Down to the most minute detail, she'd been ready with answers to all of his questions. She'd even mapped out the kind of advertising and distribution campaign she envisioned for his spaceship.

If toys were his only projects, he'd be a fool not to sign with her company. Unfortunately, this might be one contract she'd lose. If only she'd shown up a few months later. He really didn't believe she was anything more than she claimed to be, but it wasn't up to him to make the judgment. Gwinnett and the boys at Aerospace wouldn't be satisfied until they ran a full security check on her and it was his job to keep her occupied until it was completed.

Adrienne was glad that they were too busy consuming the delectable strawberry torte and its mound of whipped cream to converse. She needed a little time to figure out a way to wheedle an invitation from Kendrick to stay at his house. If only the Royal Pine would suddenly catch fire, explode, collapse, something. She was certain he'd take pity on her and offer her shelter. Short of resorting to arson herself, she didn't think that was going to happen.

"This is really a wonderful place," Adrienne commented, gazing with admiration at the pewter chandeliers, linen-draped tables and natural wood walls of the dining room. The two-story resort sprawled unevenly along a ridge. From the outside, it looked like a huge, log hunting lodge. But the inside, though still retaining a relaxed, comfortable atmosphere, was elegant.

"These people can't all be locals. How did they all find out about this place?" she asked, revealing her surprise at the number of guests filling the dining room.

"Word of mouth, I guess," he supplied. "As I understand it, Laurel Lodge has been in operation since the turn of the century. It caters especially to families. The food is excellent and the countryside beautiful around here. The rooms are very nice, too, and there are a number of cabins scattered around the grounds with more privacy."

"Do you speak from experience?" Adrienne teased, but felt a twinge of unexpected jealousy.

"I only know what Dovie told me," Kendrick supplied. "This is the first time I've eaten here. Shall I see if they have any vacancies so we can find out if she was right about the rooms?"

"No," Adrienne immediately negated, feeling a rush of heat to her cheeks. Her all-too-quick imagination proved her worst enemy as she envisioned what she'd discover if she shared a room with Kendrick. The only thing they'd notice would be the bed—if they even got that far.

She'd just been devoured by a pair of wicked green eyes, and she knew their owner wasn't interested in making a study of the lodge's decor. She'd gotten a sample of Kendrick's lovemaking earlier and knew that a night in his arms would be a night to remember, but the timing was all wrong. If she went to bed with him, he could construe it as a bribe to ensure his signing with Lang.

To Kendrick, the delightful blush that rose on Adrienne's cheeks was more satisfying than if she'd accepted his invitation. She couldn't have faked that response. Though he was convinced of her innocence, he'd sound pretty foolish if he tried to present her blush as proof to a skeptic like Gwinnett.

In an attempt to put Adrienne more at ease, Kendrick relayed all he knew about the hotel, as if his proposition had been only a joke. He ended with, "People come here to get away from the hustle and bustle of the city, do a little hiking, a lot of relaxing. Things like that."

"I can understand the appeal for some of the older couples," Adrienne admitted. Looking around the room, she noticed that one section was occupied by teenagers and the college set. "I'm surprised to see so many young people. Kids that age usually crave excitement. I shouldn't think they'd find too much of that up here."

"You'd be surprised what the mountains have to offer," Kendrick returned, finishing his torte and settling his tall frame more comfortably on his chair. Seemingly entranced by the swirling cream he stirred into his coffee, he remarked absently, "We manage a little excitement in these hills. Sometimes even enough to keep a city girl like you happy."

Adrienne chose to discount any innuendo in Kendrick's last statement and was able to successfully control her body's reaction to the excitement he seemed to generate just sitting still. However, she knew firsthand that there were other kinds of excitement in "them thar" hills—especially on lonely roads in the middle of the night. She wondered what he'd say if she told him she'd been captured by an "alien."

They'd concluded as much business as possible tonight. So far, she'd been supplying all the information. She decided this was as perfect a time as any to get a little information out of him that had nothing to do with toy manufacturing. She hardly expected him to confess that he was testing spaceships, but if she were subtle enough, maybe she could catch Kendrick off guard.

She looked furtively around her. "Some of the excitement I've heard about doesn't make me want to stick around and experience it first hand."

"Really?" he queried, lifting one brow.

"Hattie May Carson says Hubbard's Mountain is haunted," she whispered cautiously, as if she expected a ghost to appear if she spoke too loudly.

Gulping his coffee down to prevent sputtering, Kendrick stared at Adrienne in disbelief. When he felt in control enough to talk, he scoffed, "Don't tell me our local perpetuator of mystic tales has you believing all that stuff."

Intentionally acting nervous, Adrienne toyed with her silverware. "Well...of course not," she got out, seemingly embarrassed. "I'm sure the strange noises and lights she claims to see on the mountain have some logical explanation. I mean...they certainly aren't the 'haints' she calls them. They're probably just optical illusions, meteors, airplanes or swamp gas or..." She let the rest of the sentence hang.

"But?" he prompted, the teasing brightness back in his eyes.

"Science doesn't explain everything," Adrienne defended quickly, knowing she sounded like a wild-eyed devotee of ufology—exactly how she wanted Kendrick to see her. "Some highly respected scientists now believe in the work done by parapsychologists and even that there are UFO's.''

"Do you?" Kendrick grinned with an enthusiasm that could only be compared to a mischievous boy stringing a superstitious girl along.

Good, she thought. "I believe in keeping an open mind. All the people who claim to have seen a UFO or...or...an alien can't be crazy." She shuddered, bit her lip and pretended to look out the window beside their table as if she were searching for answers to her own private dilemma.

For extra emphasis, she added in a shaky whisper, "Do you think they're all loonies? I mean...maybe some of those reports are true."

With nothing but the black of night on the outside and the light reflecting against the inside surface, the window was almost a perfect mirror. She watched Kendrick's profile for a response to her distress. She got one.

He was laughing at her. He might have covered his mouth with his hand in a nonchalant gesture but she knew he'd done it to literally wipe the smile off his face. She'd like to do that for him. If she'd had any doubts of his duplicity in that horrific experience, she didn't anymore.

How dare he enjoy her fright! She wondered how frightened she'd have to pretend to be before he took pity on her and revealed the truth. A stubborn streak prompted her to keep up her act and find out. Surely he had enough humanity within him to feel remorse for having knowingly perpetuated her anxiety.

The feel of his hand covering hers made her turn to face him. "Adrienne." He sought for a serious tone, trying desperately to keep the laughter out of his voice.

It was terrible of him to enjoy her discomfort over what she imagined she'd seen, but he couldn't help himself. She was so damned cute and her suspicion of him was so obvious. Despite his qualms and a resurgence of guilt, he had no other choice but to continue stringing her along until Gwinnett gave her his stamp of approval. "I think there are many things yet to discover about our universe but I'd be careful about believing people like Hattie May."

He gave her hand a little squeeze. "If you're finished, I think I'd better get you safely tucked into the Royal Pine before the 'haints' come out for the night."

"You really think this is all a lot of foolishness, don't you?" Adrienne demanded, affronted.

"Not all foolishness," he relented as he pulled out her chair. Taking her arm, he escorted her out of the dining room. "Just the part about the 'haints.'"

"So you do believe in UFO's," Adrienne persisted.

"Let's just say I'm willing to keep an open mind, too," he returned as he guided her through the doorway and out to the parking lot.

They talked little on the return trip to Rocky Bottom Hollow. Adrienne's thoughts were occupied with the problem of how to get Kendrick to invite her to stay at his house. She rejected every idea. The only one that wouldn't cast suspicion on her real motives would involve hopping in bed with him. She'd already informed him she didn't trade her body for contracts.

Adrienne considered lovemaking the ultimate intimacy of two people who cared deeply for each other. She wouldn't sacrifice her morals just to get a peek at some secret space project. There had to be another way.

She supposed she could act as if she was too frightened to stay alone at the Royal Pine. She discarded that idea. He'd probably just laugh again. She crossed her arms over her breasts and let out a disgruntled sigh.

"What was that for?" Kendrick asked.

"Oh nothing...I...ah...was just yawning," she lied.

"I'm that boring?"

"No, you're not boring at all. Quite the opposite," she complimented, then forced a yawn. "I just didn't sleep too well last night."

Thank you, Kendrick thought silently, because she'd just provided him with the perfect cue. "I don't imagine the Royal Pine has the most comfortable beds."

"No, they don't, but on top of that I got to bed really late." Adrienne leaned her head on the seat and closed her eyes.

"Big night in Rocky Bottom Hollow?"

"Hardly. I went to Elkins for dinner and took in a double feature. It was past midnight when I got back." From beneath the sweep of her lashes, Adrienne glanced at Kendrick. He didn't even move a muscle. Darn! What did she have to do? Spill out the whole story, accompanied by a suitable show of hysteria to get some reaction from him?

"What did you see?"

Adrienne paused. *I saw a green-skinned monster with one blue eye and one green eye and I think he works for you.* Instead, she told him about the films.

"You must be a real science fiction buff to sit through a double feature of two old movies like that," he commented. No wonder she'd been so scared. She must have thought Gort had come down to get her.

"I am," Adrienne confessed. "I never pass up a chance to see one, no matter how many times I've seen it before. Even knowing what's coming up, I get just as scared the second or third time around."

He chuckled and turned briefly to grin at her. "Get bad dreams, too?"

That's what you'd like to believe, isn't it, you sadist? "Sure, that's part of the fun."

"You're a nut, Adrienne Castle."

She would have loved to tell him what he was but settled for a resigned, "So I've been told." She nestled herself a bit more comfortably against the plush seat. Her fatigue wasn't completely feigned. She really was tired.

"You don't have to stay at the Royal Pine." Kendrick reopened the topic he'd been foolish enough to let slip away.

"I didn't notice any other place," Adrienne replied sleepily.

"You could stay at my house." He braced himself for her refusal.

Perfect, Adrienne thought, but she knew better than to appear overanxious—and she wanted some ground rules. "That might not be a very good idea, Kendrick."

They were back in Rocky Bottom Hollow. Kendrick parked his car in front of her unit. Turning to her, he said, "I promise to behave myself. It'll save you driving back and forth if our negotiations take several days."

She opened one eye and gave him a skeptical look.

To sweeten the invitation, he dangled, "You could use my observatory at night and maybe you'll spot a UFO."

"Now you're teasing me."

"Guilty," he admitted, then tried a different tack. "Look, you'd be doing me a favor if you moved into my house for the rest of your stay."

"How so?"

"You saw the amount of food Dovie prepared for lunch. She does that every meal. You'd help make at least a dent in it and I wouldn't have to suffer through all those leftovers." He patted his flat middle. "To say nothing of the pounds I've gained since she started feeding me."

If he thought he'd gained weight, he must have been very thin when he arrived on the mountain, Adrienne thought. There wasn't an ounce of excess fat on his body. It was absolutely perfect.

She was about to blurt out exactly what she thought about his body but caught herself just in time. "I doubt I'll be much help, but you've played on my sympathies. Besides, I covet your bathroom."

Kendrick laughed in understanding.

"I'll move." She held up her hand when he leaned toward her. "But not until tomorrow. I'll settle up with Hattie May and be up there in the morning," she explained firmly. "And, it's only for convenience— understand?"

"Understood."

His agreement came so easily, Adrienne was worried. However, when he escorted her to the door, he barely touched her and she was admittedly disappointed when she stepped inside the cabin—alone. "It's probably for the best," she remarked as she stripped off her clothes and got ready to go to bed. "If he'd kissed me, I don't think it would have stopped at that."

Moving into his house even for a few days could be a mistake, she warned herself as she plumped the flat pillow. Nothing will happen, she reasoned with innate optimism, but memories of his kisses and caresses were the subject of her dreams as she tossed and turned all night on the lumpy mattress.

Six

———

Adrienne was amazed by the changes in Kendrick's guest room. Either he or the Hubbards had gone to a great deal of trouble between the time Kendrick had dropped her off at her motel last night and this morning. A fluffy yellow comforter and matching pillows were on the bed. Books, knickknacks and several plants lined the previously emptied shelves, and a welcoming bouquet of bright pink peonies stood in a vase on the bureau.

Leander Hubbard, a tall wiry man with blue eyes and sparse steel-gray hair, had greeted her at the front door. Evidently he'd been told to expect her, since he'd immediately picked up her luggage and started for the stairs, but Adrienne hadn't been able to tell if he approved of her coming or not. Like Hattie's son, Billy Lee, Leander didn't have much to say for himself. After placing her cases on the floor, he'd told her that he would inform Kendrick of her arrival, then walked back down the stairs.

Left on her own, Adrienne was tempted to make a quick survey of the master bedroom but she didn't know how long she had before Kendrick joined her. If he caught her nosing around in his room, he'd definitely come to some very wrong conclusions. She wondered what evidence she might find there to support her theory about him. Somewhere in this house was proof that Kendrick was involved in a secret government project and she was bound and determined to find it.

She was just hanging the last of her clothes in the closet when Kendrick appeared in the doorway. "Getting settled in all right? Will you be comfortable here?"

She knew he wasn't asking about her state of mind, which wasn't the least bit comfortable, not when he looked as if he wanted to devour her. Needing some defense, she lifted a pink angora sweater off a hanger and draped it over her shoulders, hoping to enhance the less than adequate protection of her flowered silk blouse.

"Compared to the Royal Pine, this is the Ritz," she managed lightly, trying not to stare at a massive pair of shoulders beneath a kelly green sport shirt, and the trim hips under his unbleached cotton slacks.

He didn't need to wear green to highlight those startling orbs of his but his shirt did exactly that. Today they were the color of emeralds and she felt the weight of his gaze like precious jewels nestling warmly between her breasts. Adrienne swallowed convulsively and tried to control her erratic breathing, but couldn't prevent the instant tightening of her nipples.

Why did Kendrick's looks have to be so potently male? Why couldn't she stop staring at him? His waving blue-black hair gleamed in the sunlight, a disobedient curl flicking over his tanned forehead. A tiny white bandage stood out on his freshly shaven jaw and in his hand he carried the largest yellow rose she'd ever seen.

He made no move to enter the room or give her the flower and she suddenly realized that he was just as nervous around her as she was around him. She stared pointedly at the rose, stifling a tiny giggle when he snapped out of his trance, abruptly aware of her expectant gaze.

"This is for you." He thrust out his hand. "Her name is Summer Blaze."

"*Her* name?" Adrienne stepped forward to accept the flower. "I didn't think roses had gender."

Whatever she'd expected, it wasn't the husky laughter that erupted from his chest. "That's how ignorant mankind is about the world it lives in. Nothing this beautiful could be anything but female."

"So you don't believe what science tells us? That plants are usually both?"

"Scientific facts are based on observation. I've observed that my roses are temperamental, delicate, mysterious and gorgeous—the same traits present in a beautiful woman." He smiled fondly at the yellow bloom she still hadn't taken from his hand. "She's a lot like you, Adrienne. She lights up my garden just as you have brightened my day."

She was entranced by the crinkled laugh lines around his eyes. He studied her mouth and his smile swiftly died away. When she grasped the stem of the flower, he let go.

Then, very carefully, so she wouldn't be pricked by the thorns, he wrapped his fingers around her small hand. "I promised myself that I wouldn't press you, that we'd stick to business today, but I'm going to break that promise."

He cupped her chin in his palm so she couldn't look away. "Please say I can kiss you, Angel. It's all I've thought about for an entire sleepless night."

Empathizing with the hunger she saw in his eyes, Adrienne still felt she had to resist. She didn't want to, but she was afraid that if she didn't, he might turn around and condemn her motives as he had last night in the car. "I don't think that would be very wise, Kendrick. We wouldn't stop with a kiss and any involvement would compromise Lang's position in our contract negotiations. I can't afford an affair with you."

Something frightening flared in his eyes and was transmitted to her through his gaze. Startled, Adrienne tried to back away but even though he'd dropped both hands to his sides, she couldn't seem to move. The look on his face was disturbing, compelling, absolutely mesmerizing. "Kendrick?" she gasped uncertainly.

"I will show you all my designs," he vowed fiercely, spacing his words for emphasis. His voice conveyed an awesome power yet was oddly quiet. "I will read every word of your contract and negotiate in good faith. My decision to accept or reject your terms will be based on my own best interests and whichever way I decide, you won't be able to change it no matter what happens between us personally."

Adrienne didn't know what to say but she found herself nodding solemnly. Her eyes were very large, her complexion white, and even without touching, she felt his powerful presence surrounding her.

He was so big and she had never felt smaller or more vulnerable. "I . . . I wasn't questioning your integrity, Kendrick, just trying to safeguard my own."

"Listen to me, Adrienne," he ordered quietly, taking the rose out of her limp grasp and flinging it onto the bed. "I'm going to say something to you I've never said to a woman."

The sweater she'd draped defensively over her shoulders was removed with the flick of one wrist.

For Adrienne, the meaning of the phrase, "Having one's back up against the wall" had never been clearer. She stepped back and felt the cool, smooth surface of the pecan paneling through the thin material of her blouse, but no matter how hard she pressed against it, she couldn't fade into it. Whatever was coming, she was helpless to evade.

Kendrick took up his stance in front of her, leaving her enough room to tilt her head up to see him but not enough to slip past him. "Did Greg tell you that I used to be a pararescueman?"

Adrienne was thrown off balance by the unexpected query. This was the something he'd never discussed with a woman? Wasn't his stint in the air force common knowledge?

Perplexed and more than a little frightened by his grim expression, she instinctively knew it wasn't a good time to delve into his reason for asking. She also didn't see any point in lying. "Not Greg but his wife, and she also told me you retired three years ago because of an accident."

If anything, his features became even more tense. When he spoke again, his tone was flat, his voice hoarse and stilted. "What else did Phyllis say about me?"

"Nothing much," she evaded. "She told me where you were living and I took it from there."

"Then let me tell you more about the man you're involved with."

Before she could make the protest that automatically sprang to her lips, Kendrick declared harshly, "Oh, yes, you are. Be honest with yourself. You've been involved with me since the moment I carried you off my bridge."

Mentally, he added, *And I was involved with you even before that.* Since he couldn't tell her that, he caressed her with his eyes, letting her see what he felt. He couldn't seem to find the right words and could only hope she would acquiesce to his silent appeal.

"I can't deny the attraction, Kendrick," Adrienne acknowledged eventually, having the sense to know she'd never get out of the room if she didn't admit at least that much. She didn't like the position he had placed her in, either physically or emotionally, and her vexation was apparent. Her brown eyes were smoldering, her lips taut, as she continued flatly, "I'm not saying I'm going to act on it, however. With that in mind, is there still something you feel I should know?"

"It's more like I've got to tell you so you'll see where I'm coming from," he corrected.

"So tell me." Adrienne could see by his clenched jaw that he didn't like her flippant tone and once he got into his speech, she would have given anything to take back the remark.

"The air force...they spent one hell of a lot of money to make me into a...a well-conditioned machine that could perform on command," he began haltingly. "I know how to endure killing heat and arctic cold. I can swim for miles in waters with waves a hundred feet high. I can climb mountains, find my way across endless deserts and dive to the depths of the ocean. That might sound conceited but sometimes the only reason I survived when others didn't was that I had the self-confidence to believe that I could."

He took in a deep ragged breath, then continued. "Three years ago I watched my best pilot and closest friend, Cabe Hubbard, die trying to rescue me from the deck of a burning oil freighter. There was an explosion that blasted his copter out of the sky and threw me into the water and, by some fluke, to safety. I was injured badly but luckily, a few minutes later, a Coast Guard cutter who had answered the freighter's SOS picked me up. That day marked the end of my career in the service, but unfortunately it didn't cut off my memory. I've seen more death and destruction than you can imagine and even though that part of my life is over, I still can't forget."

He hesitated as if unsure whether or not he could go on, his eyes on people and places from another time. His jaw worked without producing any words but then, after several moments, his teeth clamped shut and he came back to the present. "I moved here because I wanted to live in a world that existed without the constant threat of danger. Cabe brought me with him to visit his folks on one of our leaves and I felt such peace here on this mountain. It's a healing place."

He cleared his throat, then dredged up the painful words. "So many people...almost everyone I've cared about have been snatched away from me. I was getting phobic about it and I needed to protect myself from feeling that kind of hurt even one more time. Then you came...."

With all of her heart, Adrienne yearned to ease the suffering she saw on his face, the agony in his beautiful eyes. She could also see how difficult it was for him to reveal all this to her. Now she knew where the vulnerability, the loneliness she'd sensed in him came from. She felt if she moved at all, tried to touch him, he'd break down completely and the need to share his pain would be lost as he struggled to retain his pride.

For some reason Kendrick had chosen her, a virtual stranger, to listen as he poured out feelings she was sure no one else had ever heard. Knowing that, nothing was going to prevent her from being the best listener he could ever possibly find. "Then I came," she prompted gently.

He nodded. "I know this sounds crazy but you're only going to be here for a few more days and I'm just no good at playing games. I know that's a real failing of mine but I can't be any other way."

"I don't like playing games either, Kendrick, not with people," Adrienne said, and that inspired the first smile she'd seen since he'd started speaking. "Go on, please. I'm listening."

"Okay then," he continued with more certainty. "Something has been missing in my life and having you here has pointed out what it is. Surmounting a challenge means nothing if you don't have anyone to share it with. Whatever the personal cost, you've got to take risks or you may as well stop living."

"I'm not sure I understand what you're trying to tell me," Adrienne said in the long pause that followed.

"You were right, we're not stopping with a kiss. I want to make love to you," he stated bluntly. "I feel something for you that I can't explain but I know it goes way beyond lust."

"Oh Lord," she got out flatly, immediately dropping her head to make a lingering study of his shoes. Kissing was one thing, but becoming his lover was quite another. How in the world had things progressed to this point?

"Look at me, Adrienne," Kendrick advised tenderly, touching her for the first time since he'd backed her up against the wall. He cupped her chin and brought it up. "I swear I'm not handing you some kind of a line or trying to work on your sympathies. We've got less than a week to find out what we need to know about each other and that means cutting through all the usual garbage that normally precedes making a commitment."

"Going to bed with each other doesn't sound like commitment to me, Kendrick," Adrienne pointed out. "Business aside, what happens if a week from now you decide that your feelings were only lust after all?"

"I'm willing to risk it since I don't think that's going to happen," Kendrick said firmly. "I ache with wanting you, and I'm pretty sure you want me just as much. Can't you trust me not to hurt you?"

Adrienne was overwhelmed by guilt. He'd just bared his soul to her, unaware of the ulterior motive she had for staying in his house, and now he was asking her something that required her total honesty. What should she do? She did want him—ached with wanting him—but that didn't mean she should succumb to the temptation he offered.

She worried her bottom lip with her teeth as she tried to sort through her scattered feelings. Things were happening much too fast. Then she considered what he'd just told her. Life wasn't worth living if one never took risks, he'd said, and that was a philosophy she'd adhered to all of her life, except in the case of intimate relationships.

It wasn't that she was stingy with her affections, but she could never give less than her all. She treasured and thrived on affection but needed to have it returned. If Kendrick was to be believed, he was beginning to care for her just as she found herself caring for him. Was that enough to risk doing what he was asking?

Adrienne's lips curved in a soft smile as she gave in to the longing that had plagued her from the first. "I'm known as a very trusting soul, Kendrick."

His answering smile was one of the sweetest gifts she'd ever had. "I'm known as a cynic. Maybe together we can work out a healthy compromise."

"Maybe we can," she agreed and stepped willingly into his open arms.

Their mouths met in mutual hunger, as if there could never be enough time to draw all they needed from each other. Adrienne's body called out in invitation to know his, to feel the warmth of skin against skin. She pressed against him instinctively as his hands moved down her back to cradle her hips. She did want him, wanted to spend hours discovering and being discovered.

Kendrick could feel her trembling. He crushed her against him and she seemed to grow softer wherever he touched. He could feel a weakness in his own limbs as he thrust deeply into her mouth and knew he could never get enough of her.

Kendrick swung her off her feet and carried her out the door, down the hall and into the room Adrienne had recently thought of entering on the sly. She quickly tossed that image out of her mind, fearing Kendrick might sense her inner anxiety. She was willing to chance a relationship with him, but it wouldn't get off the ground if she admitted what had prompted her agreement to stay in his home. Once she'd helped to rid him of some of the cynicism he'd warned her about, she could tell him about her suspicions.

"You're lighter than a parachute," Kendrick said as he strode swiftly across the polished floor, heading for a king-sized bed. "And no harder to carry than my duffel bag."

"You sweet-talkin' man, you." Adrienne batted her lashes and cooed up at him. "Tell me more."

She smiled at his sheepish expression, then laughed as he gazed down at her and proceeded to murmur some extremely lurid flattery that quickly turned her complexion a becoming shade of pink.

"You'd better hope that blush covers every inch of you, Angel," Kendrick whispered in her ear. "Otherwise you won't be able to hide those lovely attributes I've just praised."

"If that's your idea of succinct, heaven help me if you get flowery," Adrienne retorted breathlessly as Kendrick swept aside the patchwork quilt that covered his huge bed, then laid her down on cool sheets. Kendrick had eyes for nothing but her as he reached for the top button of his shirt but he noticed that Adrienne wasn't looking at him. She was surveying the room. Maybe it was just as well.

Adrienne was astounded by her surroundings. The room was amazingly beautiful. As in all other parts of the house, Kendrick's bedroom gave the impression of vast open space and light, and had a wide variety of growing plants. She'd thought the atrium was the ultimate in modern design but his bedroom went beyond it. With the exception of the handmade quilt, everything was ultramodern.

The vaulted ceiling rose majestically to the skylight over the atrium and a huge multifaceted window behind the bed acted like a collection of prisms and refracted the sun's beams in all directions. A galaxy of miniature stars in every color of the spectrum danced across the bed.

Adrienne held up her arm, fascinated as the tiny lights flickered on her skin. It was like being showered in stardust. She gazed around the room at the suspended colors that gave even the most ordinary object a celestial aura.

In a far corner of the room was a circular stairway that led up to a trap door, each step bathed in a different colored light. It looked like a staircase to heaven.

"What's up there?" she asked curiously, and pointed with one finger.

Her eyes became dreamy as she conjured up all sorts of possibilities for the hidden room on the third floor. "Is that the part of the house that looks like a castle battlement from the outside?"

Seemingly unaware of the garments Kendrick was flinging off, Adrienne's overactive imagination took hold and she asked, "Or does that door lead to a dark tower where you imprison any poor maiden who might displease you? Will I languish forever there if I should offend thee, sir?''

Kendrick wasn't in the mood for her playful questions and was somewhat annoyed that she no longer seemed to be as passionate as he felt. He was standing before her in nothing but his briefs and she was playing make-believe with the attic.

"That's where I house one of my telescopes," he informed her brusquely as he reached for one of her small feet and slipped off a shoe. He wanted to get her first sight of his scarred chest out of the way, but she hadn't looked at him once since he'd laid her down on his bed.

"That must be great," Adrienne enthused, unconsciously lifting her other foot so he could remove the second shoe.

"Any night you want to, you can go up there to observe the stars. I asked my parents to buy me a telescope once but with six kids, they didn't consider it a necessity. I didn't blame them since they paid for ballet and music lessons, a piano, and lots of other things, but I never got over wanting one. I love looking at the stars and wondering what might be out there."

"You can use mine whenever you want," Kendrick promised, becoming concerned about his technique. The last time he'd reached the point where the woman in his bed was minus her shoes and blouse and had her skirt unzipped, he'd had her undivided attention. It had been so long, he must have gotten rusty.

Slowly, erotically, he began pulling her skirt down her legs. Her body was putty in his hands as he removed her remaining clothes but her mind was still elsewhere. "Can we look through that huge one out in the observatory, too? Tonight maybe?" Turning her face toward the skylight, she noted, "It looks like we'll have clear skies if those clouds don't amount to anything."

Kendrick was about to explode with unquenched passion and she was determining weather conditions. He knew he'd moved fast and he could understand her playing for time, but this was ridiculous. He was insulted and more than a little hurt.

"Maybe this will get your attention," he growled as he rolled her beneath him, trapped her head with his hands and speared his tongue into her mouth.

When Adrienne was finally allowed to come up for air, her insides were quivering with pleasure. She managed to mutter shakily, "You had my attention all along. It's just that your house is so interesting. I grew up in a standard two-story Colonial and this place really knocks me out."

"I'd rather it was me who knocks you out," Kendrick complained, thinking if the two of them ended up together, he'd often be called upon to pull her pretty head out of the clouds and place her dainty feet back on the ground. He could think of some very enjoyable ways of doing so and that brought him some solace.

He rolled to one side and propped himself up on his arm. His green eyes glittered down at her as he looked at her face. "It's not very flattering to find that the woman you want is more interested in the architecture of your house than in making love to you."

"I'm sorry, Kendrick," Adrienne said, gnawing on her lower lip as she stared at his shoulders and chest. She'd been wrong, so terribly wrong. Kendrick had been in an accident, a very bad accident and the damage had required plastic surgery.

Kendrick stiffened as he watched her expression change from one of desire to one of... What? Pity? Repugnance? He couldn't tell which, but it wasn't passion that clouded her eyes.

He forced himself not to move, not to flinch as her eyes took in the wide patches of discoloration from the skin grafts on his lower chest, the silver scars left by the surgeon's scalpel on his shoulders and upper thighs. This was the moment he'd been waiting for, the moment when he'd know if the risk he'd taken was worth it.

As he'd feared would happen, his anxiety won out over his courage. Cursing himself for being unable to face her rejection, he closed his eyes. He should have warned her, told her that his body wasn't any woman's idea of attractive. Part of him had been glad that she hadn't been watching him as he'd gotten undressed, but another part wished she'd seen what she was getting before they'd gone this far.

At first, he thought he was imagining the light caresses, until he felt the morning air cooling his damp skin. Then he felt the sweet searching of her mouth, the healing yet sensual moisture of her soft lips as they kissed him. Her touch became less tentative, then completely unafraid as she stroked his shoulders, the discontinuous line of hair that extended from his breastbone, down his stomach to widen at the juncture of his thighs.

Adrienne's hands explored the heavy muscles of his legs, not caring that the bronzed flesh that covered them was marred by the symbols of his valor. She could guess what was behind his waiting attitude, but as far as she was concerned there was no reason to wait. She thought him beautiful, his streamlined body magnificent with its scars proclaiming his dedication to duty. With the sparkling colors of the rainbow radiating off his skin, he seemed like a sungod who could call forth all the powers of the universe.

"Love me, Kendrick," she begged in a whisper as her fingers idled down his strong legs.

Kendrick groaned, arching his back as he reached out for her. He brought her to him, his heart thundering against her soft breasts. His relief was so great he was afraid he might cry out in gratitude to the supreme power that had blessed him with this incredible woman.

The feel of her slender arms wrapped tightly around his middle lent him the courage to voice his anxiety. Once he'd heard her response, he'd never have to speak of it again. "I'm not a pretty sight. I'm sorry I didn't warn you."

Adrienne pulled back slightly in order to look up at his face. "It wouldn't have made any difference to me if you had, Kendrick. I think you're the most gorgeous specimen I've ever seen and if you don't kiss me again very soon, I'm going to have to take matters into my own hands. I want you very, very badly."

Kendrick's gaze was adoring but his voice was amused. "Never let it be said I don't give a lady what she wants." His white teeth flashed as he placed one hand on either side of her head and drew her mouth up to his.

His thumbs stroked the delicate bone structure of her cheeks as he kissed her. It was a telling kiss that grew ever deeper, speaking of the pleasure to come. Lips still fused with hers, he slid his hands down her throat to her shoulders, his fingers loving every inch of her satiny skin.

"You're so tiny," he murmured hoarsely against her mouth, then he lifted his head to gaze down her body. "I can practically span your waist with my hands."

Adrienne felt his rough palms clasp her, his fingers meeting in the small of her back. His hands were large and strong, and she reveled in the feel of them as they slid slowly upward. She gasped as he sat up, lifted her off the mattress and slid her on his lap. With her legs straddling his waist, her buttocks nestled between his thighs, they were chest to chest.

Her brown eyes were wide and unblinking as she watched him place one palm beneath each of her breasts, his thumbs gently pushing inward as his fingers pushed up. She felt as if she were suffocating with the force of erotic feeling and her lips parted on a shattered breath. Never had she seen herself this way, viewed a man's possessive hands in dark contrast with the ivory skin of her bosom.

They were seated in the wide beam of magical light that shone through the large window and every curve of her flesh was showered in slivers of gold, gilded for his delectation. She didn't know if the movement was deliberate or not as he shifted and her breasts were brushed by the sun. They were soothed by the warmth, then fired to throbbing need as he kissed each pink tip.

Kendrick stared at the delicate twin blooms flowering in his palms. "Precious. You're so precious." Before the words were completely out, he was drawing one nipple into his mouth, relearning the sweet taste that enhanced his wild craving for her.

Overwhelmed by the pleasurable feeling of his tantalizing lips and tongue, Adrienne let her head fall backward, her neck no longer capable of holding it erect. She sucked in her breath as he reached her other breast.

Kendrick felt as though he'd had this room designed specifically for this woman and this moment in time. Her special beauty was highlighted by a shower of diamonds. Her skin was as translucent and fiery as an opal, her eyes like dark, shimmering amber and her hair spun gold. She was a fairy creature and he her reverent consort.

Adrienne couldn't prevent her instinctive moan as Kendrick's hand slipped down her body and cupped between her legs. "Please," she pleaded, her thighs clenching spasmodically as his fingers, gentle and knowing, sought and found her with unerring accuracy. The blissful torture went on and on and was made even more acute by the feel of his arousal surging beneath her and the cascade of colors that magnified each motion.

Adrienne yearned to give him the same pleasure and the yearning gave her an unexpected strength. She pushed at his chest and he fell backward. Swiftly, she straightened her legs and came down on top of him. Inserting one silken thigh between his, her breasts crushed against his chest, she kissed him, moved sinuously upon him until he was gasping for breath.

Kendrick curved his arm around her shoulders and reversed their positions. He rained kisses all over her face, her throat, then back up to her mouth, his tongue delving deeply as he felt her legs clasp his thighs. Carefully, he sank into the soft, miraculous part of her that awaited him.

Neither of them had enough control left to go slowly. It was as if they had an innate knowledge of each other's special rhythm, an instinct to move for the greatest mutual pleasure. As one, they lost themselves in the wonder of each other.

No matter that he'd known her for so short a time, Kendrick acknowledged that the reason he could give and receive in greater proportions than ever before was that he was falling in love with this woman. Adrienne took a few seconds longer to reach that conclusion, but neither of them was willing to admit it. Instead, they sailed together on the wave of their feelings and unselfishly supported each other as the overpowering currents pulled them to the final crest.

Seven

Arms folded beneath his head, Kendrick reclined indolently against the pillows of his bed, thinking of the tiny fawn-eyed woman who had just drained him of all power to move. The sun had moved away from the window and the colors no longer sifted into the room, but he'd never forget how fantastic they'd looked sparkling upon her skin. He would have thought the past hour a particularly erotic dream if not for the sound of a feminine voice lilting above the rush of water in the shower.

Adrienne had been in his arms, she was real, not a will-o'-the-wisp he'd conjured up from the magical lights, nor a fairy princess who'd materialized to cast a spell over him. Though his limbs felt as if he'd been drugged, he felt more invigorated and alive than he had in years. He blessed the fates that had made their coming together possible. But for a child's toy, the therapeutic hobby that had saved him from a case of terminal boredom, he might never have met her. He shuddered to think of how much he would have missed.

An insistent buzzing brought the outside world into the bedroom. Frowning, Kendrick pressed a button and the wood front of the headboard rolled up to reveal a console of buttons and a small phone. He lifted the phone onto his chest and picked up the receiver. "Sloan here."

"I hope to hell she was worth it!" Tanner Gwinnett barked into Kendrick's ear.

Kendrick bit back an instinctive retort and sat up straighter on the bed. "Since when did my private life become your concern?" he finally got out, his lips twisting. If he didn't know better, he'd have suspected that the head of Aerospace security had somehow managed to bug his bedroom and had monitored the activities that had just taken place.

"Anything that jeopardizes this project is my concern," Gwinnett relayed stolidly. "Your trusting nature has precipitated my making a judgment call, Sloan. We're flying everything out, today. Hank's got a few things left to load then we're ready to take off. That woman's already wormed her way into your bed. God knows what she'll accomplish next."

"Damn it!" Kendrick shouted, then quickly clamped his mouth shut as he glanced at the open bathroom door. He could hear the shower running but there was still a chance Adrienne might hear him if he didn't keep his voice down. "What the devil are you talking about? How many times do I have to tell you she's not connected to Trenton?"

"I don't operate on gut feelings, Sloan, only facts. We're taking no further chances." Voice calm, he continued, "Taking that woman into your house is just asking for the kind of trouble we don't need at this stage of the game. It's my job to safeguard the project and that means keeping every shred of information that might help Trenton out of her reach."

As if he couldn't help himself, Gwinnett deviated from his usually dogged manner of speech and lashed out in frustration, "Damn it man! All of us get horny. If you needed a woman so badly why couldn't you have just said so? I could have set you up with one who wasn't working for the other side."

Kendrick gripped the receiver hard, as if imagining his fingers wrapped around the security man's throat. "Your concern for my well-being is touching, Gwinnett, but I choose my own women," he drawled sardonically. "I'm convinced Adrienne Castle is no more or less than she says she is. I already told you how she located me."

"Your buddy down in Pensacola might have decided it was worth his while to give her that information on you," Gwinnett persisted, then complained, "And you didn't even wait long enough for us to find out."

"That's because I already know." Kendrick was charged with righteous anger. "Greg Robinson is a good friend who isn't on anyone's payroll. Adrienne's tie-in with Trenton is just a coincidence and so was her presence at the test site. She didn't fake her reaction. She actually thought she'd seen a UFO, and that I was some kind of creature from outer space."

"And pigs fly."

Kendrick was getting annoyed with Gwinnett's condescending attitude. The man always sounded as if he were placating a naive, absent-minded professor. Kendrick was sick of it. "My toys are the only things she's after," he vowed angrily.

"I might have fallen for that if they had been all she got," Gwinnett said crudely. "Face it, Sloan. You've been sucked in by a pro. You're not geared to handle this kind of thing so I can understand how it happened, but I won't stand by and watch the whole project go down the tubes. Aerospace has a lot of money invested here and to safeguard our position, I'm taking matters into my own hands. You agreed that everything pertaining to the security of this project would be under my jurisdiction."

"Yeah, yeah," Kendrick sighed in resignation, but his resentment was clear. "And that cloak-and-dagger mind of yours has concluded, albeit erroneously, that Adrienne Castle's a threat. Even if you were right and she is working for Trenton, I don't see what you're so afraid of. I'm committed. Trenton can offer me all the money they want but I've already been signed, sealed and delivered to Aerospace."

Not for the first time, Kendrick regretted the altruistic notion that had prompted his decision to sell his ideas to a private company. He'd wanted to get his lifesaving devices out of the lab and onto the backs of pilots. In order to speed up that process, he'd needed a lot of up-front money and a company with political clout. He'd checked out both Trenton Industries and Aerospace Limited, the two most renowned names in a highly specialized field, and had chosen the latter because their corporate policy seemed to indicate they put humanitarian considerations ahead of profits. He was beginning to think he was wrong and that both companies operated in the same ruthless manner.

Until Adrienne's arrival, he'd been annoyed by Gwinnett's zealous approach to security but now the man was behaving like a real fanatic. He took his work much too seriously and himself even more so. His ego wouldn't allow him to believe that anyone could do the job better, or that anyone not trained in security could have a valuable opinion. He was like a stubborn bull-dog with a bone, unwilling to let go until he had evidence to refute Adrienne's story.

Gwinnett's next words showed how sure he was that evidence would be found. "Up until the other night, we were positive you were our best-kept secret. After witnessing our test, the woman's probably already told Trenton that there's no way they can buy in and that it's too late to change your allegiance. The only thing they can do now is steal the suit, your designs, or some other refinement they can discover we've got that they lack."

Patronizingly, Gwinnett added, "When you've been in this business as long as I have, you learn to suspect everybody. Our sources tell us Trenton's right behind us with their own design and they've got the facilities to produce the flight suit a lot faster than we can. I'm going to make damn sure the Castle woman can't find a thing to give Trenton the edge."

"Right," Kendrick growled sarcastically, realizing there was no way he was going to talk Gwinnett out of his plans. "When do you take off?"

"In five minutes, and it's up to you to keep the woman occupied so she doesn't suspect what we're doing."

"You got it," Kendrick said shortly, then slammed down the phone.

As Adrienne stepped from the shower stall, she heard the call of a bird. Startled, she hesitated then shook her head. The jungle atmosphere of the bathroom had to be sparking her imagination. Convinced there was no one with her but the lush ferns, big-leafed plants and flowered vines, she reached for a towel. She dropped it when the birdcall came again.

Looking overhead, she saw nothing. Turning slowly, she peered intently at the heavy foliage surrounding the etched glass shower. She could detect no flutter of wings or bright plumage, yet the sound of birds calling to each other seemed to fill the room. Then it stopped abruptly.

"Next you'll be expecting Tarzan to swing down from one of those vines," she muttered as she picked up the large bath sheet and wrapped it around herself. She bent at the waist and started to wind a second towel around her head. The sound of a drum beat, distant, heavy and erotic, made her stand straight, and whirl around searching for the source.

"Care to join me?" Kendrick invited silkily from the sunken tub.

Before Adrienne could form a response, other instruments joined the drums and the room resounded with primitive music. There must be speakers secreted in every corner of the room. Making love with Kendrick on a bed radiant with colored sunbeams had been magical, but the scene spread before her now was nothing short of erotic. Her appraisal of yesterday had been correct. The tub was a hidden pool in a tropical rain forest.

Spellbound, Adrienne moved across the room, unconsciously timing her steps to the beat of the music. Finding her voice at last, she said, "This is absolutely pagan."

Kendrick laughed. "I know. Come in, let's go native together." He plucked a large, purple orchid from the vine clinging to the rough rock wall. Holding it toward her, he suggested, "You'll only need to wear this."

Adrienne's nervous giggle dissolved into a low, throaty laugh. "What are you wearing for the occasion?" she asked, knowing full well he was wearing absolutely nothing.

"I couldn't find my size in a fig leaf," Kendrick answered with a flash of white teeth.

The waterline came to midchest on him as he lounged against an inflated bath pillow. Clear, save for the patches of tiny bubbles that formed at the rippling surface, the water concealed not an inch of the power and virility immersed within its swirling depths. Adrienne felt her skin flush and tingle at the image of that masculine body joining with hers again.

As if he knew exactly where her thoughts were, he remarked, "Clothes will be unnecessary for the next hour or..." His gaze wandered down her face, studied her mouth then meandered lazily across the bared flesh above her towel. "Make that the rest of the day."

Adrienne's mouth opened then closed. As much as the junglelike decor of the bathroom suggested that she and Kendrick were alone on a tropical island, Adrienne knew that was far from the truth. There were other people to consider, prople she didn't want to shock by spending the day in wanton dissolution with Kendrick, as tempting as that thought was.

Prompted by her conservative background, Adrienne was hesitant. "What about Dovie and Leander?"

"They're on the way to visit Dovie's sister for the day."

"But...but," she hedged, still uncertain of the rightness of giving in to the desire coiling in her body. "We do have some business to discuss and—"

"We can talk here," he coaxed. "Deals are struck on golf courses, over drinks, on yachts, why not here? The Japanese do it all the time."

He laid the orchid on the edge of the pool, reached behind a plant and extracted a loofah sponge and a bar of soap. His eyes twinkled and the corners of his mouth twitched as he added, "Think what a clean deal we can negotiate."

It was a ridiculous pun but Adrienne couldn't help laughing. "And you had the nerve to call me a nut last night."

"Just trying to convince you I'm a clean-cut, all-American boy," Kendrick shot back, enjoying himself. He hadn't been part of this kind of foolish humor since...

He closed his eyes, waiting for the painful memory to drive a spike into his gut as it always did when he was reminded of his childhood and early youth. Today the pain wasn't as sharp as usual. The joy in recalling happier times lasted longer and the despair was hazy.

He opened his eyes and looked at the towel-draped woman hesitating to take those last few steps to join him. Adrienne. She was no bigger than a wood sprite and yet she'd single-handedly taken on the dragon that had tortured him for half his life. To ensure her victory, he dropped the sponge and soap and picked up the orchid.

"Come, my Titania," he invited again, his voice a gravelly whisper. "Let me crown you queen."

Remembering Shakespeare's *A Midsummer Night's Dream*, Adrienne pointedly eyed the deep purple flower in Kendrick's hand. She stepped backward and, taking poetic license, dramatically implored, "I fear thee, Oberon. Wilt thou squeeze the juice into my eyes that I might fall in love with the first thing I see?"

In the same vein and with equally histrionic flair, Kendrick responded, "You wound me, fair maiden. I plot no mischief."

"Hah!" Adrienne disdained with a haughty nod of her head. "So you would want me to believe, but I know a knave when I see one."

"'Modest doubt is call'd the beacon of the wise,'" he quoted back. She was a delight, the first woman who had matched him step for step both physically and intellectually. He enjoyed this kind of sparring almost as much as making love to her.

"Oh ho!" Adrienne hooted, her eyes glowing mischievously. "You admit it, you blackguard! You had no intention of discussing business in that tub."

"Did you?" he fired back with an utterly audacious grin. Sobering only slightly, he invited her once again, "Come. We'll get around to business in due time."

"I fear thy thoughts stray wide of commerce, sir. If I do share thy bath, I beg thee not to press thy suit without honor."

"As you can well see," Kendrick drawled, "I have no suit, but press thee I will."

It was a blatant statement of his intent. Entranced by the verdant glow in his eyes, she couldn't pretend resistance any longer. Throwing caution aside, she unwound the towel from her head, fingercombed her hair then smoothed it away from her face. She slid the towel slowly from her body in a smooth motion and let it slither to the floor.

Wearing nothing but a smile as old as Eve, Adrienne stepped into the little pool and slowly lowered her body into the warm, bubbling water. "It's a Jacuzzi," she stated the obvious, her voice so full of astonishment the sensual mood was shattered.

Treading the water and reveling in the invigorating motion of the bubbles surrounding her bare skin, Adrienne breathed in the scent of eucalyptus rising from the steaming water. In awe, she exclaimed, "This is *some* hot tub!"

Kendrick's laughter was louder than the music. Gone was the enchantress whose mysterious smile and seductive walk had stimulated his body to near-explosive tension. In her place was a wide-eyed ingenue. He wasn't sure which one he loved more.

She might match him in wit, Shakespearean scholarship and physical appetite, but in mood changes she outstripped him. Adrienne, an original, a woman beyond measure. He moved across the pool, needing to be close to her.

"This should go right here," Kendrick said as he tucked the orchid over one of her ears. He closed his hands over her shoulders and gently pulled her to him. Intently studying each feature in turn, he stated, "And this should go right—" he lowered his face until his lips were a hairsbreadth from hers "—here," he finished and settled his mouth over hers.

His tongue flicked at the outline of her lips and with a tiny sigh, Adrienne opened them to him. Kendrick answered her sigh with a low moan then took all of her mouth. Gentle and slow at first, his tongue caressed the honeyed warmth it touched.

Adrienne wound her arms around his neck. The buoyancy and swirling motion of the water brought her breasts against his chest then pushed her away with the lazy rhythm as his tongue danced in her mouth. Soft flesh brushed against hard until gradually the tempo increased and the water lapped dangerously at the edges of the pool.

"Adrienne," Kendrick breathed as he released her mouth. Cradling her face in his hands, he touched the orchid behind her ear, then pressed kisses across her forehead, down her cheeks and onto the throbbing pulse point of her throat.

Her voice shaky, Adrienne asked, "If that's the kind of kiss that accompanies a single blossom, what do you give with a lei?"

He chuckled wickedly against her skin as he clamped his hands around her waist and lifted her until her breasts were level with his mouth. Between flicks of his tongue against her nipples, he asked, "How are you spelling that last word?"

Adrienne caught her breath as he took one nipple into his mouth. "Kendrick..." His name trailed off to a breathless whisper and she forgot the admonishment she'd meant to deliver for his audacious question—nor did she need an answer to her own. Her body felt weak and melting, while at the same time a tension began to build deep within her.

He treated each rose-tipped mound equally, worshipfully, before slipping one arm beneath her legs and the other behind her shoulders. He kissed her between words as he rose from the water with her cradled against his chest. "Despite rumor to the contrary, this is a hellish place to make love."

"A man trained to swim miles in the ocean ought to be able to handle a hot tub," she teased.

Undeterred by her taunt, Kendrick stepped from the tub and started toward the bedroom. "The heat and motion of the water can get to you," he told her. "Another few minutes and we both would have been limp rags."

Adrienne resisted a playful refutation of his statement. Kendrick was all hard muscle and aroused virility. She ran her palm along his shoulder and across the hair of his chest. "Let's stay in the jungle," she pleaded huskily, nipping lightly at his earlobe.

"The floor's too hard and cold." He strode through the doorway and to the bed. "Close your eyes and pretend," he directed as he placed one knee on the bed and maneuvered them both down to the soft mattress.

His mouth on hers silenced any protest and soon Adrienne was lost in a swirling haze of sensations. She ran her hands over his shoulders and down his back, slick with the water droplets still clinging to his skin. His hands were just as busy skimming over her, brushing her dry with the heat of his palms.

With the exotic music swelling and building to a passionate crescendo, the scent of eucalyptus and orchids filling her nostrils, Adrienne had no trouble imagining that they were indeed making love in a tropical jungle. Kendrick left her mouth to cover her cheeks and neck with tantalizing kisses while his hands stroked and caressed her breasts before wandering downward. One large palm covered her flat stomach while his other hand teased her inner thighs, coming close then retreating from the center of her desire.

Skimming her hands down his hard flanks, Adrienne responded in kind. Closing her small hands around him, she drove him nearly over the edge of reason. "Guide me, now," Kendrick requested as he cupped her buttocks and lifted her toward him.

A need as primitive as the drum beats surged within Adrienne and she granted his wish, which was also her own. Together they gave themselves up to the power of primal desire. Faster and faster, higher and higher they soared until they reached that final moment of blinding ecstasy.

Kendrick relaxed upon her, his face damp against her neck. Adrienne encircled him with her arms, stunned by the intensity of the experience. She had never felt such deep satisfaction, could not believe it had happened. She was now irrevocably tied to a stranger who had erased all of her misgivings and had taken her to a new world.

"'Other women cloy the appetites they feed, but she makes hungry where most she satisfies.'" Kendrick muttered Shakespeare's description of Cleopatra without thinking as, unbelievably, he felt himself grow within her.

It was past noon when Adrienne stepped back into the shower. Kendrick had told her he'd use the shower off the kitchen and then prepare their lunch. She was grateful to him for having left her alone because she needed time to make sense of all that had just happened.

What kind of a spell had he cast over her, she wondered as she dried herself and hurried down the hall to the guest room. As soon as she entered, her eyes lit upon the yellow rose lying in the middle of her bed. Still fresh and lovely, it seemed symbolic of her relationship with Kendrick.

Her feelings for him were as new and fragile as the petals of the rose. Like the rose, would their relationship shrivel and die in a short time? Or, with proper care, would it endure and bloom? She didn't know. At this point, she wasn't sure of anything—not even of herself.

She knew Kendrick was an inventor but he must also be a wizard. She wasn't the type to hop into bed with a man at the crook of his little finger, but that was all Kendrick had to do to make her quiver with need for him. For the past year she'd been working very hard and had taken little time to play. Perhaps this wild fling she was having was just a natural result of the grueling schedule she'd been keeping.

As she stepped into a pair of slacks, she denied that cowardly rationale. Her social life hadn't been all that empty. She'd had plenty of opportunities to indulge her sexual frustrations if she'd felt the need—but she hadn't felt it. It was Kendrick. There was something about him that drew her, kindled a passion she had never known, and thrust her into a world where there were no moral questions. Everything she did with him seemed perfectly right.

"Are you coming down?" Kendrick called from the first floor. "Or do you want me to bring a tray up there?"

Since she knew she had no resistance to him, Adrienne hurriedly buttoned her blouse and started out of the room. "I'm on my way," she called down the stairs. Maybe the kitchen would offer some safety. At least it didn't have magical lights and a tropical atmosphere. With any luck, she could keep Kendrick at arm's length for the rest of the day.

"Do you believe in Santa Claus?" Adrienne inquired shakily as she gazed at the cluttered shelves in Kendrick's workshop. She saw several hand-carved puppets, small wooden sailboats, plastic rockets and minirobots, all lined up in neat little rows. The gifts he'd sent to Kenny Robinson were only the tip of the iceberg.

"Why?" Kendrick flipped on a wall switch and a toy train chugged slowly through the miniature city laid out on the large plywood table in the center of the room. A whistle sounded, a bell rang, and the locomotive gathered enough speed to make it up a tall papier-mâché mountain.

"Because I'm beginning to think you're in his employ."

Kendrick chuckled at her serious tone. "Do I look like an elf to you?" He was a bit startled by her thoughtful stare and the long pause that followed. Whenever she looked at him, he wanted to pull her into his arms but in her present mood, he could see she wouldn't welcome the action. He stuffed both hands into the pockets of his jeans and waited for her to answer.

"I've never seen an elf so I'm not sure what they look like but I swear your little kingdom is just what I'd picture for Santa if he had a summer place away from the North Pole." She gestured widely, encompassing not only the vast collection of toys in the workshop but everything else she'd seen since he'd begun the tour of Hubbard's Mountain. "I've felt as if I've been enchanted ever since we met and none of this gives me any reason to doubt it.''

His only response was a maddening grin, so provoking that she shouted. ''Who are you, Kendrick? Where did you get the money for all this? You can't expect me to believe that your only income comes from your retirement benefits from the air force, yet you insist no other company has bought the rights to your toys. Right now, your being an elf is the most logical explanation I can come up with.''

He burst out laughing.

''I'm serious, Kendrick.''

He hiked himself up on a stool, placed his hands on his hips and shook his head. ''Only you would think my being a overgrown elf was logical. What's your explanation for my green thumb? I saw your face when I showed you my prize tomatoes. Have you concluded I'm also a close relative of the Jolly Green Giant?''

It sounded outrageous when put like that, but Adrienne had entertained a somewhat similar notion when he'd taken her through the large greenhouse built behind the house. Plants, vegetables and flowers of all kinds were grown without soil and had developed blossoms, leaves and edible fruit far larger than normal. He'd explained the scientific process, but it had sounded very strange to her, very strange indeed.

''Your vegetables and flowers aren't the only things that make me think you've got otherworldly connections. What about that launching pad out there?''

As they'd taken a wide path to the very top of the mountain, she'd seen a huge circular plot of ground surrounded by lights. He'd told her that it was a landing site for a small helicopter he owned, but when she asked to see it, he'd said the copter had broken down and he'd taken it to a flight mechanic in Elkins to be repaired. Once again, a perfectly logical explanation that only added to her suspicions.

"Launching pad?" Kendrick tried to control his amusement but had little luck. He decided to keep his mouth shut until she completed the barrage of questions he could see forming in her huge brown eyes. "What other nonsense have you come up with?"

"Maybe that spaceship you gave Kenny has a father that takes off and lands in that circle of blue lights rigged up outside."

"I knew you were imaginative, Angel, but now you're really reaching." His face creased in a huge grin.

"Am I?" she asked, unable to keep herself from voicing all the questions that had been plaguing her ever since she came. "What about all that junk in there?" She pointed to the large door that divided the interior of the building into two sections.

His workshop took up half the space. The other half was devoted to his interest in astronomy. He'd explained that the instruments and graphs, the computers and monitors only served to increase his knowledge of the universe, but she had the uncanny feeling that there was far more to it than he was telling. That huge silver disk on the roof might provide better reception for his TV, but it could have other more disturbing uses.

"Is your computer really waiting for messages to come in from outer space or does it send them?"

She had yet to mount the stairs to the huge, domed observatory but could imagine what kind of reaction she was going to have when she did. It would be incredible, just like every other part of this self-sufficient, unique, and private world he'd created for himself in the span of three short years.

"I thought you must have acquired all this from the government, perhaps sold them some space-age marvel you invented, but you haven't," she declared. Trying to cover the tiny note of hysteria she heard in her voice, she emitted a dry laugh. "I'm not going to find one shred of proof that you're involved in some secret government project so I can just give up trying, can't I? I've gotten myself involved with a..." She couldn't say it but was well on her way to believing that Kendrick wasn't human.

"Oh, Angel," Kendrick sighed. He didn't know whether to kiss her or shake her. "You could have asked. No, I'm not working for the government. I have a perfectly legitimate and very 'this-worldly' source of income. My parents died when I was seventeen and I inherited a lot of money. I used a great deal of it to buy the mountain and build my house and workshop."

Hopping down from the stool, he walked over to her and placed one arm over each of her shoulders. Staring down into her eyes, he continued, "I have a lot of interests—astronomy and botany are two—but I'm also into robotics and what Dovie calls my gizmos. I own about twenty patents, mainly on safety devices I invented to make pararescue easier, that provide a comfortable income. Satisfied?"

Eight

Adrienne stepped away. "No, I'm not satisfied!" she retorted shrilly. "Ever since I stepped over the state line strange things have been happening to me, and I'm tired of thinking I'm losing my mind. I know you're behind everything I've seen or done since I got here. Why don't you admit it?"

Kendrick was taken aback by her anger and concerned that she seemed on the verge of panic. "I'm not admitting to anything until I know what you're talking about," he said soothingly, even if he was now quite familiar with how her mind worked and what she was afraid of. He had half a mind to ignore Gwinnett's warnings and tell her everything but there was too much at stake, and he still didn't have verifiable proof that she wasn't a corporate spy.

Something very strange had been happening to him, too, since she'd come into his life. He was actually thinking about love, marriage and starting a family. He barely knew the woman and yet he was happily entertaining a fantasy of her sharing his life, having his babies. He, who had once chosen a career with a high mortality rate, was envisioning growing old with her.

"Come on, Adrienne," Kendrick coaxed, gently sliding his arm around her shoulders. Her shudder magnified his guilt. "Tell me what's bothering you."

Face averted, Adrienne poured out the tale of her abduction by an alien, the fear she'd experienced, followed by her later assumption that she hadn't been the victim of some monstrous visitation but a witness to a government test. She went on to explain why she now believed that conclusion to be wrong, which left her stuck with the first one.

"I...I think I'm falling in love with you, Kendrick," she confessed. Tilting her face upward, she looked him squarely in the eye and announced, "I think I have the right to know if you're a Martian or a Venusian or something."

She hesitated a moment, her brown eyes searching his for understanding and answers. In a rush, she blurted, "I'm not prejudiced or anything and I know you aren't going to hurt me, but if you tell me you're not from this world, I've got to make some adjustments in my thinking."

Kendrick had never been so sure of anything as he was now of his love for her. In her typical style, which was both straightforward and convoluted, this sweet woman was telling him that she could accept his being inhuman if he would tell her the truth. How much longer could he stall without ruining everything good between them?

"I'm falling in love with you, too," he stated softly, hoping the admission would help ease her mind. When she found out the real explanation for what she'd seen she was going to be madder than hell, and he wanted her to remember what he'd said to her today. "I'll admit that I'm involved with something that has led you to these crazy conclusions but I'm not free to tell you what it is. I'm just a man, Angel, and nothing you've seen on Hubbard's Mountain can't be easily explained. Trust me."

"Trust you?" Adrienne repeated and it wasn't a question she was asking of him but of herself. She stepped out of his arms, putting more than physical distance between them. She took another survey of his workshop and her eyes settled on the life-size robot that stood like a suit of armor in the corner. "What can that thing do?"

"Charlie is programmed to fetch my tools."

Could she trust a man who had created a robot named Charlie to wait on him? There was nothing alien about having a robot—uncommon perhaps, but not proof of his citizenship in another galaxy. She'd read about similar ones, she reminded herself. Robots were being used more and more by industry to perform simple tasks. It was just startling to come face to face with one in somebody's home.

"And that?" She pointed to a clawlike contraption that dangled from a heavy wire strung along the ceiling.

"That's a mechanical arm. When I need to make an adjustment to my work that requires completely steady hands, that comes in handy."

"Oh," Adrienne replied dully, feeling a bit foolish but still fearful. "Every home should have one."

"This isn't my home, it's my workshop," he reminded. "Actually, I share it with Leander. He's an expert wood-carver and makes all the wooden toys. He and Dovie are sort of the Mr. and Mrs. Claus of these mountains. They started making and distributing toys to needy children in these parts several years ago."

"Can I see the observatory now?" Adrienne wasn't ready to turn her back on her fears until she'd seen what was up in that cinder-block dome. The explanation of the workshop was plausible, but she wasn't ready to trust that the toys weren't a cover for something else. As for the observatory, if the only thing he'd installed was a powerful telescope, maybe she'd be able to accept all his other explanations, but if it looked as if he had set up two-way communication with the stars, she was getting out of there.

Kendrick reached for her hand, swearing softly when she tucked them both in her pockets and waited for him to take the lead. "You're really something, you know that?" he bit out in frustration as he started up the stairs. "You must drive your family crazy. Have you suffered delusions all your life or did they start recently?"

"They started when a baked potato jumped out of a spaceship and almost landed on top of me. And I'm still not too sure you weren't at the controls when it happened."

Kendrick started to say something, then stopped himself. He stood there for several moments, debating whether or not to come clean. She wasn't with Trenton; he knew she wasn't. What harm would there be in telling her?

"What's the matter, Kendrick? Are you hiding a rocket launcher up there, or a few lizardly relatives?"

Kendrick shot up the remaining three steps to the small iron-railed landing. "I'm hiding a three-meter reflecting telescope that cost me a fortune." A whoosh of dry air hit him in the face as he opened the wide door, and he detected the change in his left eye. "Damn!"

He closed the door immediately and dropped to his haunches, carefully studying the green tile floor. His fingers searched gently, feeling for the fragile, gel-like object he'd just lost. "Don't come any closer," he warned. "You might step on it."

Adrienne froze partway up the stairs. "What? Are there little furry creatures running around in there?"

"For God's sake!" Kendrick shouted, glaring at her. He'd had just about enough of this alien garbage. His eyes bored into her face, making it clear he'd run out of patience.

"Oh my God," Adrienne whispered as she stared back at him. With him in a crouched position and herself on a lower step, she and Kendrick were face to face on the same level. There was no way of misinterpreting what she was seeing. He had one clear blue eye and one that was a shimmering emerald green!

Her panic grew to the weight of an anvil crushing her chest but she forced herself to look more closely at his skin. Did it have a slightly greenish cast? Since the interior of the observatory was a pale olive she couldn't tell, but it didn't really matter, not any more.

"You're him! Or it! I knew it!" She swallowed a scream and turned back down the stairs, scrambling down them so fast she almost fell. On the ground floor, she ran as fast as she could for the door.

Kendrick was right behind her but she made it outside before he caught up. Adrenaline surged through her limbs, lending her a speed that overcame her short stride. Like the wood sprite he'd called her, she sped down the graveled path, running so fast her feet barely touched the ground.

Kendrick studied his quarry with an expert eye. Should he try for a flying tackle and risk hurting her or go for a modified version of the fireman's carry? She was beyond reason, beyond the point where he could talk her out of her fright, so the only thing left for him to do was keep her from hurting herself. If she didn't slow down she was going to break her neck.

He closed in on her, passed her and whirled around. Lowering one shoulder, he caught her at the waist as she slammed into him. He clamped one arm across her thighs and started walking toward the house. "You're not going anywhere until you hear me out."

Instead of the hysterical response he expected, she gave him a sharp dig between the shoulder blades. "And if I don't choose to listen, you'll use those hypnotic powers you've got to bend me to your will. I knew I wasn't in my right mind when I went to bed with you. I've been a helpless victim of some kind of mental control this whole time."

"Shut up." Kendrick gave her a sample of the physical control she was currently under by tightening his grip. "I swear if you say one more word about me being an alien, I'm going to tie you up and gag you."

To Adrienne, his threats were oddly reassuring. Neither his words nor the action he threatened to take denoted superhuman powers. What kind of a Martian would bind and gag when he could probably vaporize her with a flick of one finger? He also could have used his telepathic powers to keep her from running.

Chances were high he wasn't an alien, but still...those eyes. Those incredible, strange, different-colored eyes. She knew of people whose eye color didn't match but never had she seen such a dramatic difference. "What would you have thought if you'd been me? Your eyes are..."

"I'm a heterochromeairide," Kendrick snarled in exasperation and before she could leap to another wrong conclusion, he explained, "And that's not the name of another planet but the medical term for different colored irises."

"Makes sense," Adrienne allowed. "You can put me down, Kendrick. I'll listen."

"Not on your life," he retorted grimly.

Resigned to her position, Adrienne settled in for the ride. She propped her elbows against his back and cupped her head in her palms. She was recovering fast and busily began to assimilate the facts as she knew them. If Kendrick didn't work for the government and he wasn't an alien, then what kind of trick was he playing? Less than twenty-four hours ago, she'd suspected him of being a practical joker but what he'd done to her wasn't the least bit funny and went beyond the confines of decency.

"Is life so dull up here that you have to get your kicks from scaring people?" she asked with a return of temper. "Or is leaping out of trees the only way you can get a woman?"

"I think you know better than that," he growled.

"No, I don't," she snapped back. "You drugged me that night, didn't you? How desperate is that?"

She could feel the muscles of his back go rigid. "I was desperate all right—desperate to get you out of a state of shock."

They reached the house and he carried her inside, not setting her down until they were in the living room. "Sit!" he barked, pointing to the leather couch.

Adrienne did sit down but not because he had ordered her to do so. Her legs were trembling with reaction. "Am I supposed to thank you? You were the one that caused my shock in the first place."

Tucking his hands in the back pockets of his jeans, Kendrick began to pace. He strode over to the fireplace as though he'd forgotten Adrienne's existence, and placed one foot on the raised hearth, staring into the empty grate. Finally, as if he'd come to a difficult decision, he slowly turned and came back to the couch. Giving her an intense look, he released a long sigh.

Then, crouching in front of her, fingers linked between his knees, he studied the floor for several moments. "Okay, I'm going to explain this whole damnable mess."

Adrienne waited, sensing that it would be wise to keep silent.

"What you saw the other night was me testing a new flight suit I designed. I've been paid thousands by Aerospace Limited for the development of a lightweight, nonflammable, radio-equipped suit that will aid in the rescue and survival of downed pilots."

He reached for one of her hands, absently playing with her fingers as he went on. "As it happens, Trenton Industries is in the process of developing a similar product but mine has certain innovations that make it superior. It's a highly competitive field so security had to be strict. Then, right in the middle of our final test, you show up.''

"So? Why didn't you just tell me that? I would have understood and certainly slept a lot better with the truth.'' Another thought struck her. ''That's what you thought I was after! Your flight suit. But why? Why would you think that? I told you I was from Lang Manufacturing. We make nothing but toys.''

"Lang is a division of Trenton Industries. You must know that. It was too much of a coincidence that you arrived at such a critical time in our experimentation. It was a logical conclusion.''

Adrienne stared at him for a long time, noticing that he was having difficulty meeting her eyes. There was a lot he still wasn't telling but she was prepared to bide her time until she'd been given the whole under-handed story. ''Lang was a small family-owned company,'' she informed stiffly. ''It was solid but the only way it was going to get any bigger was with the backing of a conglomerate like Trenton. We were purchased last year but we still operate very independently. Except for members of the board, everybody else at Lang goes about their business the same as always.''

"Our investigation only began yesterday and nothing conclusive has turned up yet. I'm sure that—''

"Investigation? You've been investigating me?'' she asked quietly but was inwardly seething.

Kendrick swallowed hard but forced himself to look into her eyes. Her features were blank, giving no clue to her feelings but at least she seemed willing to listen to reason. ''With so much at stake, we had to go by the book. I tried to convince security that you weren't connected to Trenton, but if you knew Tanner Gwinnett, you'd realize he's about as easy to convince as a mule. All I could do was tell him I'd keep an eye on you until you were cleared."

Adrienne could feel the rage inside her surging for release. She had never felt so betrayed, so used. Kendrick's gracious invitation to come to his house, to his bed... "You bastard!"

She stood up so fast that Kendrick was caught off balance and fell backward. He landed heavily on his backside. Momentarily stunned, he watched helplessly as Adrienne rushed toward the stairs. "What's wrong now?"

Adrienne ignored him and continued her flight up the steps. She couldn't get out of there fast enough. Knowing he would come after her, she slipped the lock in the door as soon as she was inside the guest room. She dragged her suitcase and garment bag from the closet, then began emptying the hangers and dresser drawers.

"Unlock this door!" Kendrick shouted as he pounded on the wood. "Be reasonable, Adrienne. None of this was my idea."

With remnants of her clothing still hanging out of her case, Adrienne snapped it closed. Suitcase in hand, garment bag over her shoulder, she marched to the door and unlocked it. "Step aside," she ordered imperiously.

"Won't you please listen to me," Kendrick pleaded. "You're overreacting."

"Where is the flight suit, Kendrick?" she asked coldly.

"Gwinnett and his crew flew it out this morning. If it were still here I'd be perfectly happy to show it to you and prove that I trust you."

The rigid set of Adrienne's features became even more tight. "So that jungle fever you suffered this morning was to cover the sounds of the great get-away. Right?"

Kendrick groaned. Whichever way he answered, he was damned. He reached for her, then dropped his arms back to his side when he saw what she was holding out to him. A shaft of pain, stronger than any he had known, cut through his body.

With a flip of her wrist, Adrienne flung the yellow rose at his feet. "You can keep this as a reminder of what a fool I've been."

Kendrick closed his eyes. He was losing her and there was nothing he could do about it.

"I never want to see you again," she ground out tersely, then swept past him and down the stairs.

Adrienne accomplished the drive back to Pittsburgh in record time. The beauty of springtime in the mountains was lost on her as she concentrated on the highway rolling out ahead. Each mile closer to Pittsburgh was another mile further away from Kendrick Sloan and the biggest mistake she'd ever made in her life.

Imaginative revenge plots occupied her thoughts for the first fifty miles. She hoped the sun would stop shining over his mountain and his solar-heated home would turn into a refrigerator. Then he and all those hideously beautiful plants of his would freeze.

She hoped he'd test his flight suit in outer space and get lost in a black hole. She hoped lightning would strike his disk receiver and he'd be forever denied communication from the outside world. Let him be totally cut off from humanity—the world would be better off!

Or maybe the opposite would be a better curse. She could take out ads in all major publications announcing that the "hunk of all time" lived on a mountaintop in West Virginia and she'd provide a map to get to him free of charge. That would certainly pay him back for treating her like a tramp and for the despicable way he'd maneuvered her into his bed.

He'd been laughing at her the whole time, encouraging her fantasies and keeping her occupied while he waited for a security check on her to be completed. "You'd be doing me a favor if you moved into my house," she mimicked in a sarcastic rendition of Kendrick's smooth line that had resulted in her moving out of the Royal Pine. She'd granted him a favor, all right! *Her favors.*

In the tradition of James Bond, he'd taken a suspected female spy to bed, to keep her from learning things he didn't want her to know. She wished she had been a spy and had stolen all the secrets of his precious flight suit. She wished she could keep him from earning one penny on his latest patent.

Kendrick Sloan was no pauper, not by a long shot. He had enough money from all his other patents, he probably wouldn't even miss the earnings from this one. Nor would he miss the money he would have gained by Lang Manufacturing's marketing of that cursed little spaceship!

He was out nothing while she'd be lucky if she still had a job. She'd have to absorb all the expenses for this harebrained trip, but that was nothing compared to the price she'd paid in heartache. She was going to continue paying that for a long time. Not in dollars and cents but in pride.

Kendrick Sloan had no scruples. She couldn't get over how he'd played on her sympathetic nature and gullibility. Every lie he'd told her came back and she repeated them out loud.

"You're so beautiful. You brighten up my day. I feel something for you that I can't explain."

He certainly would have had a rough time explaining that going to bed with her was the best possible way to keep her distracted. And oh, how distracted she'd been! Like a mindless idiot she'd believed he was not only the most wonderful man in this world, but even that he'd been born of another.

Looking back on it, she wondered how he'd managed to keep a straight face for so long. Men! And they have the nerve to talk about the wiles of Eve. She had firsthand knowledge that the male of the species was just as conniving as the female, if not more.

"String 'em along. Tell 'em you're falling in love with them," she bellowed. "You can make 'em believe anything, do anything, if you're good enough in bed," she declared, almost wishing the truck driver who'd just passed her could hear her condemnation of his sex.

"Knights of the open road! Hah!" she roared when she was hemmed in by two large semitrailers on a steep incline and forced to slow down. "Chivalry died when the Round Table broke! A man will take advantage of a woman every chance he gets!"

She felt better and better as she continued to vent her anger. "Even the knights of old weren't trustworthy. Look what happened to Guinevere." From her point of view, King Arthur and that rat Lancelot had been cut from the same cloth as the King of the Mountain she'd just left.

Eventually her boiling rage degenerated to a low simmer then sputtered and died as she drew closer to Pittsburgh. A vast sense of loss and betrayal replaced her anger. All those glorious hours she'd spent in Kendrick's arms, hours when she'd given her heart as well as her body, hours when he'd made her feel like the most cherished woman in the world, had meant nothing to him.

By the time she'd turned in the car at the airport rental agency, all she wanted to do was put the entire painful episode behind her and get on with her life. *We can only learn from our mistakes,* she silently repeated the words her mother had taught her as a child. *There's a lesson in each one.* As she walked through the terminal, searching for the airline with the earliest flight to Minneapolis, Adrienne recited her lessons.

She'd never trust a man with green eyes again . . . or blue eyes . . . or especially one of each. She'd never fall in love at first sight. She'd never eat leather breeches or cracklins or anything else that could remind her of the Hermit of Hubbard's Mountain.

She had plenty of time to commit each vow to memory for she discovered that the first available flight to Minneapolis wasn't scheduled to take off for four more hours. Prepared to wile away the time with a paperback novel, perhaps become so immersed in a story she'd forget her heartache for at least a little while, Adrienne marched confidently to a newsstand. Selecting something suitable became not only difficult but nearly impossible.

The last thing she wanted to read about was somebody else's successful love life, so romances were out.

She'd sworn off science fiction for life. Adventure books were no good for the same reason. She'd just co-starred in a steamy scenario that rivaled anything Ian Fleming had ever thought of.

Eventually, she settled on a safe, nonfiction work entitled, *Planning and Forethought, The Keys to Success*. She picked up a newspaper and a couple of magazines just in case the book didn't hold her attention, then sat down on a chair near her gate.

The book didn't tell her anything she didn't already know, but it delivered the lecture she knew she deserved. It was never wise to jump in without a definite plan of action. It was best to research all angles before choosing the best method of proceeding. Plan ahead. Plan ahead. Plan ahead.

She'd wasted five bucks. She'd been getting the same tips free all her life. First her parents and then her sisters had tried to get that point across to her without any luck, and the terminology used in the book was weak by comparison. Adrienne placed the paperback down on the empty seat next to her. Maybe now, after this latest disaster, she'd finally learned her lesson and she wouldn't need that book lying around to remind her of her folly.

Experience is the best teacher. The wisdom in those words had finally gotten across. Never again would Adrienne Castle rush in where angels fear to tread! The next thing she had to do was publicly own up to her professional failure, and in private, lick the wounds of her personal mistakes. No one was ever going to find out that she'd fallen in love with a man who had no more heart or integrity than that tin can he'd programmed to fetch his tools. She held on to that thought all during her flight back to Minneapolis and was proud of herself for not breaking down until she got home.

On Monday morning of the following week, Adrienne marched into Ted Erwin's office and explained that she'd been unable to come to contract with Kendrick Sloan. In her mind, her fingers were crossed that her boss wouldn't demand to know any of the details. "We couldn't agree on the terms."

"No problem," Ted surprised her at the finish of her brief report. "I'm sure you gave it your best shot." He paused, grinned across his desk at her, a twinkle appearing in his eye as if he had some sort of secret.

Adrienne shifted uncomfortably in her seat, wondering if somehow Ted had guessed at the reasons for her failure. Impossible, she judged. She'd said nothing to indicate she'd formed any sort of relationship with Kendrick Sloan, and she'd have to be tortured before she'd admit to anyone that she'd actually thought she'd had a close encounter with an alien.

Close? She almost laughed at the pun and looked away from Ted, fearing that he'd see the misery in her eyes. She'd had a close encounter, all right, as close an encounter as two beings, human or otherwise, could have. She sighed. If she continued thinking about the intimacies she'd shared with Kendrick, she'd burst into tears and Ted would demand an explanation.

She glanced at him, realizing that he'd stopped talking and was still grinning at her in that mysterious way. She felt like Alice in Wonderland looking at the Cheshire Cat.

"Lang Manufacturing will manage and so will you," Ted finally continued. In a paternal tone, he went on, "Just look at this as a temporary setback. You never know what the future will bring. We might still get that spaceship. Stranger things have happened.''

That's an understatement, Adrienne moaned inwardly. *And having an affair with a man who I thought came from another world is perhaps the strangest of all.* "I'm afraid I don't have your optimism about ever putting that spaceship into production,'' she said instead.

"One less flying saucer on the market doesn't spell doom," Ted placated. "We'll find something else that'll be the hit of the next Christmas season. I'm impressed that even on vacation, you kept your eyes and ears open for anything new. Meanwhile, concentrate on some innovative ways to market what we've already got.''

He picked up a folder, tapped it, then tossed it across his desk. "This is a complete rundown on everything we have in production right now. Cost, sales, everything, it's all there for you to look over. I want you to decide which of our products deserve the biggest advertising campaigns, and any you think should be dropped. That should be more than enough to keep you busy for a while. Come on, Sunshine, don't look so glum. One failure does not a loser make.''

His choice of sobriquet, one he'd used almost since her first day of employment, didn't garner her usually bright response. It only reminded her of Kendrick and the way he'd claimed that she brightened his day. As far as considering herself a loser—that went without saying.

Somehow, Adrienne managed a faint smile and picked up the folder. "I'll get on these right away.''

After leaving Ted's office, she stopped to chat with his secretary, then made her way down the hallway to the cubicle she called an office. The first thing she did was toss her plants into the nearest wastebasket. They'd grown leggy and sick-looking in the window-less room and she couldn't bear to look at them. The contrast to Kendrick's lush plants seemed symbolic of his trickery and her gullibility.

Once she'd done that, she began a careful study of all the information Ted had handed her, cognizant of the responsibility she'd been given, and grateful to Ted for his continued faith in her. Over the next few days, she settled back into work, her daily routine not very different from what it had been before she'd gone on vacation. She met with ad men, planned the seasonal promotion campaigns, approved the artwork and threw herself into writing most of the copy. All that had really changed was the bright-eyed optimism that had once been her trademark.

It had finally happened. Adrienne Castle had met defeat. She'd failed to succeed in something she'd really put her heart into. The loss of the contract for a new toy had been bad enough. In her mind, it was a career defeat even if it hadn't been labeled that way by her boss. Ted seemed to think an occasional setback was all part of the law of averages. "You win some, you lose some," he quoted. Adrienne wished she could be that cavalier about it.

Perhaps she would have looked at it that way if Kendrick had turned out to be the eccentric recluse she'd anticipated. Then maybe, and it was a big maybe, she might have been able to put the whole thing behind her and could have written Kendrick off as a kook. Unfortunately, she knew exactly what Lang had lost because of her involvement with him.

The only fortunate thing about the whole affair was that no one but she understood the underlying reasons for her growing despondency. For the first time in a life of giving and receiving love, she'd been hurt, deeply and irrevocably. And with each passing day the pain got worse.

Nine

———

Three weeks later, after working very late on a Friday night, Adrienne was sleeping in late Saturday morning. She was feeling groggy when she picked up the phone on her bedside table and heard the deep velvety tones she'd tried so hard to forget. "Hello Angel."

"Kendrick!" She pushed a tangle of hair off her forehead and struggled to sit up in her bed. Mind still fuzzy with sleep, she couldn't hide the pleasure she felt at the sound of his voice. Her own voice was throaty, charged with longing as she asked, "Is it really you?"

"It's me all right," he answered huskily, but then the strain of frustration seeped into his tone. "I'm sorry it's taken me this long to track you down but, if you recall, I was right in the middle of some important business when you walked out. I couldn't get here until yesterday.'' He paused, then added, ''If you wanted to make me suffer, you sure got your wish.''

With every word, Adrienne came more fully awake and by the time he'd finished speaking, she had remembered all the reasons that she never wanted to see Kendrick Sloan again. ''You've got some nerve calling here!''

''I'll be doing one hell of a lot more than calling,'' he threatened quietly, then hung up.

Mouth agape, Adrienne stared at the phone. Before she'd absorbed what had just happened, her doorbell started ringing. Her eyes went wide with both fear and a heady exhilaration she hadn't felt for weeks. Had Kendrick been calling from somewhere within her apartment complex? What if he were standing right outside her door?

Her heart was beating so fast she felt ill. She scrambled out of bed and searched frantically for a robe to cover her skimpy, blue lace teddy. Heavy chenille wasn't exactly what she'd imagined wearing if she ever got the chance to confront him again, but it would have to do. She hadn't said half what she'd wanted to when she'd stormed out of his house, but he was going to get it with both barrels now.

The doorbell continued to ring as she pulled viciously on the belt of her robe, cinching her waist tightly. She didn't even care that she could barely breathe as she grabbed the door handle. Shaking with anger she declared loudly, ''You're the biggest, the worst...''

It took a moment for her mistake to sink in, then she squeaked in astonishment at the tall, athletic-looking blonde standing in the hallway. ''Rosie?''

''Yes, your biggest worst sister.''

"Sorry," Adrienne apologized, completely deflated. "I thought you were the paperboy. He's late every morning," she lied.

Rosie lifted a skeptical brow. "Sure kid."

"What on earth are you doing here?" Adrienne demanded, switching the subject.

"You know Mother," Rosie said, shrugging her shoulders as she stepped past her befuddled sister. "Her birthday's next weekend and she knew I was coming up for that but she couldn't take it any longer."

"Take what?" Adrienne asked, though she had a good suspicion.

"She says you're living on nothing but nerves, that you won't tell anyone what's wrong, and she's desperately worried." Rosie didn't look the least bit worried herself as she sat down on the living room couch and stretched her long legs out on the coffee table. "Am I the first one here?"

"Who else am I expecting?" Adrienne sighed, dreading the answer.

"Mother's decided it's time to gang up on you, kid." Rosie gave her a good-natured grin. "I've been elected commander and my mission is to take the youngest Castle by storm. Want to tell me what's bugging you before or after the rest of the troops arrive?"

"Good grief!" Adrienne flounced into her bedroom, calling back over her shoulder. "When are you guys going to learn I'm not a baby anymore? I can handle my own problems. I don't need my Amazon sisters to come hold my hand whenever things go wrong."

"So Mom *is* right," Rosie shouted back. "You may as well fess up, Addie. She won't call off the dogs until we've dragged the whole story out of you. It's your own fault. If you wanted to be left alone to work out your problems you shouldn't have lost even an ounce of weight, or grown those dark circles under your eyes. You've always been the runt of the litter and it never takes much for Mom to get hyper about you."

"It's not my fault I didn't get any height," Adrienne retorted. "By the time Mom had me she'd run out of inches."

"You grew out instead of up," Rosie reminded dryly. "We got legs. You got boobs."

Adrienne's snort was muffled as she pulled a T-shirt over her head. "Your big noses make up for any other deficiencies."

"They come in handy when Mom decides it's time to butt in," Rosie shot back, not insulted at all. The older Castle sisters might tower over Adrienne but they all had been blessed with delicate facial features. "She's given us marching papers and you know what'll happen to us if we mess up."

At the disgusted noise from the bedroom, Rosie went on more seriously. "Now that I've seen you for myself, I'm worried, too. You're usually up with the birds and it's almost noon."

"Since when is it a crime to be tired? I've been putting in a lot of overtime lately."

"Another sign of avoidance if you ask me."

Adrienne's heartfelt curse was lost as the doorbell rang once again. Assuming it signaled the next contender in the forthcoming rounds of chaos, she shouted ungraciously, "Since you're running this party, you answer it."

She heard Rosie start for the door as she pulled on a pair of jeans, surprised at how easily the zipper slid up. Her sister was right, she admitted grudgingly. She'd lost enough weight that her eagle-eyed mother would have noticed. She should have been more careful and not skipped so many meals.

When she reentered the living room, Rosie wasn't greeting another Castle sister but accepting a long, white box from a delivery boy. "The plot thickens!" Rosie grinned as she shut the door and turned around. "Score one more for Mother. She said it was a man."

"Cripes!" Adrienne marched across the room and snatched the box away from her uninvited intruder. Pretending a nonchalance she was far from feeling, she tossed the box onto the kitchen bar. Hand on her hip, she addressed her sister. "Sorry you can't stay any longer, Rosie, but I understand that you wouldn't want to leave your kids with Mom and Dad too long. I know how you hate having to undo all their spoiling."

"Come on," Rosie urged, grabbing the florist's box and shoving it at Adrienne. "Let's open it. I can't stand it. I'm dying to know what we got."

"We? Why couldn't I have been an only child like I deserved?" Adrienne wailed, but her curiosity couldn't be put off any longer. In the Castle household, flowers and candy sent to one daughter were gifts to all. Since in the not too distant past, she'd dug her fingers into many of Rosie's chocolate-covered cherries, she had no choice but to let her sister stand by as she opened the box.

If they were from Kendrick, it might give her the perfect opportunity to tell the whole story before Rosie resorted to bamboo sticks under the nails. Her fingers shook slightly as she slipped the satin ribbon from the shiny box. Lying in a bed of green tissue paper and ferns were two dozen long-stemmed yellow roses. A small white card rested atop the bouquet.

She opened the card and as she read what was written upon it, her eyes brimmed with tears, remembering the last time she'd seen a yellow rose. In block letters was the message, "Our first honeymoon might be over but our courtship has just begun." It was unsigned.

Hanging over Adrienne's shoulder, Rosie gasped. "Oh my, Addie. Am I glad Mother's not here to read that. You'd better tell me what's going on. Kendrick Sloan must be some kind of man."

"But what kind? That's the question," Adrienne moaned, taking the flowers with her as she collapsed onto the couch. "And how did you know these are from him?"

Rosie answered with ease. "I put two and two together. Phyllis Robinson told me what he looks like and Mom says you've been like this ever since you got back from West Virginia. Since you normally tell us far more than we ever want to know about any man you're involved with, we all figured this one was really special."

Adrienne shook her head in resignation. Her family knew her too well. "I was only with him for two days and I fell in love, really in love. It was crazy and I made a complete fool of myself."

Shoulders slumped, she began pouring out the whole miserable story. Because she found it so difficult to talk about, it took almost an hour to tell Rosie all that had happened. She held nothing back, not even her foolish assumption that Kendrick was an alien.

Rosie had the good grace to refrain from teasing her about her gullibility and was the soul of sympathy when she told how she'd given Kendrick her whole heart and how badly he'd treated it. It was both an agony and a relief to admit her feelings out loud, disclose how devastated she was that Kendrick had only been using her.

The doorbell interrupted her at a point when her tears were falling freely. Once again, it was Rosie who accepted the florist's delivery. "Are you sure he was only using you?" she asked, a doubtful expression on her face as she placed the box down on Adrienne's lap.

Sniffing, Adrienne murmured dumbly, "What is he up to? I don't understand any of this. That phone call, the flowers. You read the note. What am I supposed to think?"

"Maybe you'll get a clue if you open this and read the card," Rosie instructed gently and slipped the ribbon off the box.

This time, Adrienne found a garland of orchids—purple orchids. She blushed a fiery red and feared that the tears on her face might turn to steam. She remembered the passionate kiss that had accompanied Kendrick's giving her a single orchid and the torrid interlude that had followed. The card tucked into this exotic reminder gave her an answer to the question she had asked him that day. "With this lei, I give you everything I have."

Adrienne could feel the barriers of anger that had protected her heart for weeks melting away. If Kendrick was going to this kind of trouble to make up with her, perhaps she had judged him unfairly. There was no getting around the fact that he had taken advantage of her to protect his flight suit, yet here he was sending her flowers and love notes. Was it possible that the brief time they'd spent together had meant as much to him as it had to her?

She would have liked to be alone to consider that question but over the next hour her apartment was invaded by first one sister, then another, until all her siblings were present. To make matters worse, Marlys and Karen, the thirty-one-year-old twins, had brought along their youngest children. Sue at twenty-nine was the closest to Adrienne in age. Since she'd tried without success to have a child for so long, she refused to go anywhere without her adored infant son. And, in order for Josie, the second eldest sister, to devote all of her time to conversation, she'd brought two of her preadolescents to look after the little ones.

The conversation was interrupted every hour on the hour by the arrival of a new gift from Kendrick. As her sisters oohed and aahed, Adrienne unwrapped an expensive telescope, then a lovely paperweight that enclosed a miniature castle complete with moat, and finally a beautifully crafted gold charm shaped like a knight in shining armor.

A collective groan greeted the last. "All I got from Pat was a brass pin from Annapolis," Rosie complained. "Big deal!"

Josie chimed in, "The love of my life coughed up a wilted bunch of violets he snatched from Mom's garden. Arnie won't spend money on anything but those stupid gemstones he keeps locking away in our safety deposit box. All those gorgeous sapphires, and none of them for me."

Marlys, always Adrienne's worst critic, gibed, "Wouldn't you know! Shortstuff here, who's always led a charmed life, gets Prince Charming. I got stuck with Attila the Hun." Everyone laughed at the unfair description of Marlys' blond, muscle-bound husband who was a tackle for the Minnesota Vikings. Tough and mean on Sunday afternoons, Jim Bradley was the biggest pussycat in the family and treated his wife as if she were made of the finest porcelain.

Adrienne didn't have time to consider the ramifications of the gifts Kendrick had sent her. She was too busy running around the room serving coffee to the adults and doling out cookies to the children. To reduce the din, she dragged out the trunk of toys she kept in the closet and turned off the television whenever a pair of inquisitive baby fingers turned it on. However, her stomach did a flip-flop when the doorbell rang once more and yet another gift was presented to her. The blue velvet box was from a well-known jeweler and she trembled with anticipation as she held it in her hand.

A diamond-cut crystalline prism was nestled in the velvet. It caught the light as soon as Adrienne had opened the lid. It was as if Kendrick had caught up those fantastic light beams from his room and placed them in a box just for her. A rainbow of dancing colors flickered off the walls and bounced from the ceiling.

The youngest members of the family clapped their pudgy hands in delight as the magic spread throughout the room. Sue was the first to speak. "Good golly! What is that, the Hope diamond?"

"This guy doesn't mess around," Karen judged, blue eyes sparkling enviously. "Read the card, Addie, and if you aren't in love with this guy by now, I'm prepared to get a quick divorce from John."

"No way," Rosie interrupted at once. "I'm dumping Pat. He can have the kids and the dog. I'll take diamonds."

"You're so mercenary, Rosie," Sue admonished playfully. "The most expensive thing Larry's ever given me is my wedding band and I still love him to pieces."

Everyone groaned. Sue served as everybody's conscience, always the one to point out their misplaced priorities. Aware that she was about to be throttled, she added "However... for a bauble like that even I might sell my soul."

"It's not a diamond," Adrienne explained in a shaken tone, her mind elsewhere. Her gaze was soft and dreamy as she dangled the prism from its long golden chain. "It's even more precious."

Her sisters' teasing voices faded away as she slipped the card from the envelope. She didn't know how much more of this she could take without becoming a total emotional wreck. An image of Kendrick's face swam before her eyes, then it expanded to include his magnificent naked body showered in spellbinding light. She could feel his arousing voice vibrating against her bare skin as she read, "A reminder of the magic we shared and can share again. Have dinner with me."

He's coming! Adrienne felt a jolt of sheer panic as she glanced at her watch. It was already five o'clock. How much time did she have to get ready? An hour? Two? When he arrived, she wanted to look her best and that meant it was past time for her to evacuate the premises. She loved her sisters dearly but this was one time when they couldn't help her and would only make an awkward situation that much more difficult.

She and Kendrick had so much to say, so much to work out. His idea of courting had softened her up, prepared the way for their meeting, but she needed much more from him than his gifts and notes. He was a marvelous lover, created worlds of pleasure for her enjoyment. He played on her heart strings with the expertise of a virtuoso, but was he prepared to give his heart in return? She needed to know if they really could share the magic again or if it could never be re-captured.

This time she was going to find out everything there was to know about him before succumbing to his brand of wizardry. This time she was going to rely on her head instead of her instincts. Kendrick had taught her a lesson she'd never forget, and she was going to proceed very slowly. If he were serious, if he truly loved her, he would be willing to wait. She had to be sure that the world he was asking her to share existed outside the limits of his incredible imagination and her romantic dreams.

She bent down and picked up her one-year-old niece. "Lynnie, tell your mother she's overstayed her welcome."

She handed the child to Karen then scooped up another. "On behalf of your favorite aunt, James Michael Bradley the third, please inform the rest of this assembly that they should give me a break and go home."

Suc claimed the infant seat that held her sleeping firstborn before Adrienne got the chance. "A brick doesn't have to fall on my head," she declared in mock indignation.

"I take this to mean you're going to give Kendrick a second chance?" Rosie inquired as she got down on her knees to help the older children pick up the coloring books, board games, building blocks and other toys scattered across the floor.

"Take it to mean whatever you like," Adrienne stated airily as she strode into the kitchenette, grabbed a dishrag and began wiping the crumbs and spilled milk off the counter. "And if any of you say one word of this to Mother, I'll have your heads."

She knew her threat fell on deaf ears but she hoped her sisters would grant her enough time to prepare Kendrick to meet the woman commonly referred to as Mother Matchmaker. Each one of them had been victim of their mother's machine-gun tactics and none of them had enjoyed it. "Please let this alone until I know if Kendrick and I have a future."

Everyone spoke at once, in a hurry to reassure Adrienne that her wishes would be followed. They swarmed around the kitchen bar anxious to impart their last words of advice. None of them heard the doorbell ring or saw Karen's four-year-old daughter, Ann, run to answer it.

"Hi," she offered shyly as a much bigger man than her Daddy stepped through the door. Her blue eyes were huge as she surveyed him. "Is your name Kendrick?"

"Yes," Kendrick returned, mystified by the child's prompt recognition and intense stare. Beyond that, he was stunned by the number of people he saw crammed into such a small space, a space he'd expected to be occupied by only one tiny woman—his woman. Instead, there appeared to be a half dozen taller versions of Adrienne and several much smaller ones on hand. Only two of the crowd were male but even those were endowed with the same blond hair. *Amazing,* he thought. *I've walked in on a whole nest of them.*

"Then you belong to my Aunt Addie," Ann declared, frowning dubiously up at him. "I think you're too big for her."

"I think I'm just right for her," Kendrick stated, his deep rumbling voice bringing about an immediate silence.

A score of blue eyes and one set of horrified brown ones zeroed in on him and he instinctively took a step back. Kendrick had never seen anything quite like what happened next. If he hadn't moved aside, he would have been bowled over by a sweeping tide of women as they hefted belongings and children into their arms and rushed for the door. He felt himself blushing like a schoolboy as he overheard some of the comments they made as they bulldozed out of the apartment and down the hallway.

"Did you see that nonstop body?"

"Lord! I'd kill for eyes that color, and those lashes!"

"If Addie doesn't want him, we can divide him up between us. There should be enough to satisfy everyone."

"Uh huh, and all of it prime."

"Wait till Mother gets a load of him."

Adrienne wanted to die an instant death. She prayed Kendrick was suffering from a momentary loss of hearing but could see by his embarrassed flush that her sisters' compliments had been heard. This was the worst possible way she could ever imagine meeting him again.

Her legs refused to carry her out from behind the bar. In a soiled, wrinkled T-shirt and her oldest jeans, her hair uncombed and her face devoid of makeup, she looked like a destitute waif. He looked better than gorgeous.

Kendrick stared at her for several moments. She was so beautiful and he'd missed her so badly. Knowing he had to proceed slowly or risk losing her again, he offered what he hoped was a winning smile.

Adrienne swallowed the lump in her throat. He was close enough to see, to hear. If she took a few steps further, he'd be close enough to smell, to...touch. No, she mustn't make the mistake of touching him. Nervously, she dropped the dishrag in her hand and lifted her fingers to her throat, covering the frantic pulse beating there.

Her Prince Charming wasn't a dream but an actuality. In his crisp white shirt and navy blazer, he was the epitome of raffish charm. His shirt was unbuttoned partway down his chest and provided a view of the tanned column of throat and a glimpse of hard, hair-matted chest. Adrienne's fingers tingled in remembrance of how that hair felt over the contours of muscle. His beige slacks hugged his hard thighs and molded over taut hips and ...

"May I come in?"

Adrienne's head snapped up, hoping Kendrick hadn't noticed the direction of her eyes but he had. His smile had changed to a grin of pleasure. "You are in," she stated the obvious in a choked tone. She made a flustered gesture at the open door. "I've...those were my sisters. Kendrick...I..." She wanted to cry.

Kendrick crossed the living room, holding her with a gaze that was meant to, but didn't, put her at ease.

He couldn't hide the green glitter of his eyes that told her he still desired her. His magnetism was as potent as ever, and her resistance was just as weak. It was through sheer force of will that she held her ground.

"Thank you for all those lovely presents," she said almost in a whisper. "I shouldn't accept them."

He gave her a questioning look that was meant to be harmless but took aim on the corner of her mouth. It was as if she hadn't said a word for all the notice he paid to her statement. All communication between them was being conducted on a plane far above the mechanics of speech.

Say something, she begged silently, trying to block out what he was telling her with his eyes, his expression, his entire body. The message sent was clear. He wanted her. He was going to have her, no matter what he had to do to get her.

She had to stop him. She refused to be a willing victim once again. The first note he'd sent was a promise to court her and she was determined to hold him to it. "You make a pretty apology, Kendrick, but I'm still not sure of the motives behind it."

He looked baffled. "How could you miss them? I never meant to hurt you. Isn't it obvious to you by now that I love you? I want to marry you."

Adrienne was grateful for the counter that still separated them because it was the only thing that kept her from throwing herself into his arms. He loved her. Kendrick loved her. Her heart sang but another voice drowned out the song. Caution. Use caution. Don't let him hurt you again.

"It's obvious that you want me, but love me?" she asked in a remarkably even tone. "You don't know me well enough to love me and I don't know you well enough to marry you."

Kendrick hid the surge of triumph that swept through him. Her lapse might have been unconscious, but it told him exactly what he needed to know. As far as she was concerned her love for him wasn't in question, only her trust. If she had a logical mind, he would have pointed that out, but Adrienne was rarely logical. It was the most intriguing, frustrating and delightful thing about her.

He sat down on a bar stool and reached out his hand. "Then let's get acquainted."

After a tense pause, Adrienne agreed, "All right." She placed her hand in his and held back a joyful sigh as his fingers closed warmly over hers.

Ten

_____

We've been together every night this week and I still know next to nothing about you," Adrienne declared with exasperation as she ducked beneath the possessive arm draped over her shoulder. She stared at Kendrick as she complained, "You know all there is to know about me, all about my job and my family, but according to you, your life started the day you joined the air force."

Kendrick leaned back on the couch, his jaw going tight as he recognized the truth in her accusation. He struggled to come up with another acceptable evasion, then stopped. For the past week, he'd done just about everything but talk about his early life and Adrienne was right to call him on it.

If he wasn't careful, he was going to lose all the ground he'd gained. It was just that what he'd accomplished thus far had been so simple compared with what she wanted him to do next. To prove how good he thought her at her job, he'd signed an exclusive contract with Lang Manufacturing. To demonstrate that he was serious about courting her as she deserved to be courted, he'd wined and dined her at the best restaurants in town.

He'd taken her dancing, showered her with enough flowers to start her own nursery and more candy than she could eat in a year. To show her that his intentions were honorable, he'd forced himself to settle for a few chaste kisses at the end of each evening when the need to make love to her was driving him rapidly insane. Tonight, however, while she'd been working up her imagination, he'd been trying to think up a feasible way to get out of the promise he'd made not to touch her.

What he hadn't done, had resisted doing all along, was to assuage Adrienne's need to understand what had made him into the man he was, the man she loved. Before she'd stepped into his life, he couldn't remember how long it had been since he'd allowed anyone to delve into his feelings, probe the wounds he carried in his heart. Yet he'd already told her things he'd never revealed to anyone but Cabe Hubbard, and it had taken Cabe years to accomplish what Adrienne had managed in just a couple of days.

It still hurt to talk about Cabe, about the accident that had taken his best friend's life and ended his own career, but the pain had eased when he'd told Adrienne about it. Unfortunately, with that layer of grief less intense, the pain of other losses was that much closer to the surface. He could tell that Adrienne sensed he was still holding back.

This time, he knew she was asking him to disclose much more than he had the last time. The day she'd agreed to go to bed with him, he'd spouted some pious platitudes about taking risks and surmounting challenges, but she was the one who'd had enough courage to trust him. She deserved the same measure of faith from him and if he was such a coward he couldn't give it, he didn't deserve her.

But what if after he'd told her the story of his life, he saw pity in her eyes? What if she concluded that his need for her was only a neurotic means to regain what he'd lost? He couldn't stand it if she thought that.

His love for her had developed so quickly. He knew she was worried that his feelings weren't genuine and might not last. He didn't want to say anything to increase those worries. How could he convince her that he would have fallen in love with her no matter what the time or the circumstances?

Kendrick had been so lost in his private thoughts, he didn't realize Adrienne had left him alone on the couch until she spoke from the kitchenette. "I'm going to have some brandy," she said tightly. "Would you like some?"

"If you think plying me with liquor will get me to talk."

Adrienne took no offense for Kendrick's tone was light and teasing, the words accompanied by an endearing smile. "I've tried everything else," she muttered but could feel her annoyance slipping away. It was hard to remain angry with a man who had such a sweet smile. "My seductive ways certainly haven't gotten to you."

"Wanna bet?" Kendrick grinned, running a finger around the inside of his shirt collar. "If I hadn't made that stupid promise not to touch you until you agreed to marry me, I'd be inside you right now.''

Adrienne gulped. Her hands were trembling with the need to touch him but she managed to finish filling the second glass of brandy without spilling any. Then, holding both glasses in front of her, she carried them across the living room. Kendrick's remark had set off an alarming attack of desire, and she didn't want him to see the physical results. Her nipples were throbbing and erect, crying out for his attention. Her insides were mush.

Defensively, she retorted, "I'm beginning to think that lofty promise was just a form of blackmail.''

"Is it working?''

Oh it was working all right, but she wasn't going to admit it—not until she was positive they had much more to look forward to than a terrific sex life. In the meantime, she felt like a victim of cruel and inhuman punishment.

Each night as they'd parted company, he'd kiss her lightly with all the passion reserved for a kindly old relative. Adrienne told herself she was glad that he was giving her time to think, but she was finding it hard to concentrate on the simplest tasks. She'd turned into a clockwatcher at work, counting the hours until she saw him again, but once she was with him, she couldn't wait for the evening to end, hoping he would forget his vow before she broke down and begged him to share her bed.

Tonight, they'd eaten a casual dinner in her apartment. Dressed in jeans and short-sleeved knit shirts, they'd dined on hamburgers and french fries at the kitchen bar then adjourned to the couch to talk. Adrienne had babbled on and on about the marketing campaign she envisioned for his toys, news of her family, anything to keep her mind off sex.

When she'd run out of topics, it had suddenly dawned on her that she'd done most of the talking for the last seven days. It was ridiculous, but as far as she knew, the man she wanted to marry might very well have been hatched fully grown from an egg.

"Do you have a family, Kendrick?" Adrienne decided to press the issue as she handed him his brandy and curled up on the other side of the couch.

"What are you doing way over there?" he growled, frowning when she drew even farther away.

"I'm keeping temptation at arm's length," she replied cheekily, determination clear in her brown eyes. "Let's go over a few minor details I seemed to have missed along the way, like where were you born?"

"I don't know," Kendrick said without hesitation, resigning himself. "Not for certain. I was a foundling like you see in old movies."

"Honest?"

"Yup." Kendrick couldn't help but smile at her expression. "So I guess you'll never have any real proof that I'm not an alien. I don't know who my real parents are..." he trailed off suggestively. "Or even if they were human."

Adrienne grimaced. "How often do you plan to tease me about that?"

"How often will you let me?"

She pretended to consider the question for a few seconds, then wrinkled her nose at him. "If it's left to me, once is too often."

"Too bad," Kendrick said, cautiously shifting along the cushions to get closer to her. "I rather liked having you think that I was a super-being with incredible powers. Did wonders for my ego."

"I'm sure." Adrienne took a sip of brandy then asked another question. "So what happened to you after you were found?"

Kendrick had sidled close enough to reach for her hand. Once he was sure she wasn't planning to pull away, he placed first his glass then hers down on the coffee table. That done, he drew her into his embrace, her back against his chest, his arms crossed in front of her.

"I'm not going anywhere, Kendrick."

"Humor me, Angel," he requested as he drew in a deep breath. "This is hard."

Adrienne placed one of her hands over each of his and relaxed her spine. She could feel his breath in her hair, feel the strong thud of his heart and she knew she was in the only place she ever wanted to be. "I love you, Kendrick."

The response she got to her admission wasn't verbal but it didn't have to be. She could feel Kendrick's muscles go slack and then his heart started beating very, very fast. The next instant, his arms tightened around her until she couldn't get her breath. She was unable to prevent a soft gasp of protest and his hold immediately loosened but he didn't allow her to move and he didn't kiss her.

"I had a brother, Adrienne, an identical twin brother." Kendrick's whisper was so soft she barely heard it but then he cleared his throat and began speaking more loudly. "I'm sure Marlys and Karen have told you that there's a special bond between twins. In my case, Josh was more than a brother, more

than a friend because we didn't have anyone but each
other.''

"Oh, Kendrick." Adrienne tried to twist in his arms
in order to see his face but he held her fast.

"Let me get this out," he pleaded harshly. "It'll be
easier if I don't have to—"

"It's okay," Adrienne interrupted before he completed the sentence. "I understand." She could feel
him gearing himself up once again and she gripped his
hands hard, trying to give him the strength to tell her
something so horrible he couldn't look at her when he
told it.

"Josh and I were found in a deserted building in
Chicago. We were about three months old. The au-
thorities had to wait quite a while before determining
that our parents couldn't be found, so we spent our
first few years in foster homes. I don't remember
much about that."

His voice changed, became more animated as he
went on to tell her about Kyle and Allison Sloan, the
young couple who had eventually adopted both him
and Josh. The Sloans had no living family but Kyle
had inherited a fortune from his father's estate, and
they were anxious to provide a good home for the
three-year-old twins. Kendrick, his brother and their
adopted parents had been as close as any family could
be. They did everything together and there wasn't a
day when the brothers didn't feel they were greatly
loved.

The day before the boys' seventeenth birthday, the
family had taken off on a ski trip to Aspen. Kyle was
piloting the new plane he had just purchased. An engine gave out over the snow-laden mountains and be-

fore Kyle could recover from the sudden loss of altitude, they had crashed.

"It was so cold," Kendrick recalled brokenly. "So terribly cold and the wind, I remember the wind. Mom was killed on impact but Dad lingered on for several more hours. Josh and I got him out of the plane, tried to stop the bleeding, but we didn't know what to do and after a while he stopped screaming and just . . . slipped away."

Adrienne didn't even try to staunch the tears that were flowing down her cheeks. She wrapped Kendrick's arms more closely around her, feeling the bitter winter wind, the horror and the loss. She wanted to absorb Kendrick's suffering into herself but all she could do was listen and love him.

"We didn't know how to do anything," Kendrick bit out. The frustration, fear and desperation in his tone were as acute as they must have been that day. "We didn't dare get too close to the plane because fuel was leaking and then . . . there was this awful explosion and the whole thing went up in flames. Mom was dead but she was still in there, and all we could do was stand and watch."

Suddenly, his tone went flat and he began relaying the terrible hours and days that had followed. With only the clothes on their backs, no food or shelter, Kendrick and Josh made a mistake that would ultimately cost Josh his life. They had left the wreckage of the plane and started down the mountain. On the second night, Josh had collapsed in his brother's arms.

"We were the same height and weight, in the same physical condition but he just gave out. I...I couldn't leave him there all alone so I carried him as far as I could." Kendrick's voice broke for a moment as he relived the last minutes of his brother's life. "Eventually, I had to stop and rest and when I lowered Josh to the ground I knew he was dead. Less than an hour later, the rangers who had followed our tracks from the plane found me."

Adrienne was immediately aware of the exact second when Kendrick had forgotten she was with him. His arms dropped from around her and she was able to turn and look into his face for the first time. His beautiful green eyes were wet with tears, his face ravaged. She drew his head onto her breast, stroked his temples, whispered her love. "No more, Kendrick. You don't have to tell me anymore."

After a while, he lifted his head and offered her a weak smile. "I have to tell someone, Adrienne. I've needed to share this for years but I couldn't. For a long time afterward, I felt very guilty for not dying with them. Everyone I cared about was gone and all I had suffered was frostbite and exposure. I was only in the hospital a week."

"Your family wouldn't have wanted you to die, too," Adrienne stated softly.

"I know, but I blamed myself for not knowing what to do to save them. I was determined that if ever I was in another situation like that one, I'd know everything."

"And so you became a pararescueman, an expert in saving people's lives."

Kendrick nodded. "I joined up as soon as I recovered." Mechanically, he began to recite the code he had lived by ever since, "It is my duty as a member of the Air Rescue Service to save life and to aid the injured. I will be prepared at all times to perform these duties before personal desires and comforts. These things I do that others may live."

He made a visible effort to pull himself back together, to get beyond his emotion. "The ARS insignia depicts a blue sky streaked with a golden ray of hope and a guardian angel whose arms enfold the globe."

He reached into his pocket and handed her the badge that had once been sewn on his uniform. "You should have this, Adrienne, for that's what you are to me. You're my golden ray of hope and the angel whose arms enfold my world."

"You'll never be alone again," Adrienne promised fervently, moved beyond measure. Not even a wedding ring would bind her to him more completely than this frayed scrap of cloth. She cupped his face in her hands. "I love you, Kendrick. I'll always love you."

Kendrick searched her expression for any sign of pity but all he saw was sympathy, love and a wondrous joy. "I'll always love you," he echoed.

The birthday cake, lovingly created for Rebecca Castle, was a memory. All that remained were a few crumbs and a heap of slender candle stubs. A mountain of crumpled wrapping paper and discarded ribbon was providing entertainment for the delighted toddlers, enclosed for their own safety in a portable fence. One infant slumbered peacefully in a net-draped playpen set up beneath the shady branches of an oak tree. The older children, ranging in age from four to fourteen, were engaged in a loose and boisterous game of croquet at the back of the Castles' yard.

No less boisterous were the thirteen adults sitting around the picnic table. Teasing gibes shot across the table, Adrienne receiving more than her usual share—especially from her sisters' husbands.

"Where's this Mr. Perfect I've been hearing so much about?" Arnie asked, receiving a jab in the ribs from Josie.

"Yeah," agreed Larry and John, joining forces against the man who had apparently been the primary topic of conversation in their respective homes for the past week.

Adrienne opened her mouth several times to explain Kendrick's absence but was continually overridden by the stronger voices surrounding her. Finally, she gave up. When she'd finally allowed him out of bed this morning, reminded him of the family gathering, Kendrick said he had some pressing business to attend to, but that he'd drop in later. Considering the announcement they were going to make, she was beginning to wonder if he'd gotten cold feet about facing this wild bunch.

"Little Addie kept him away for his own safety," Pat teased. "I was going to sic the hulk on him." He nodded toward the six-and-a-half-foot tower of muscle seated next to him. Compared to the Viking lineman, even burly Pat Callahan looked small.

With a leprechaun grin, Pat punched his brother-in-law's bulging bicep. "How 'bout it Jim? You going to cream that guy for me? Rosie's threatening to run off with him and leave me all alone with that stupid mutt of hers."

Before the easygoing, handsome giant could answer, Rosie sprang to her feet and exclaimed, "My mutt! You're the one who spent all that money on a fancy English Setter that turned out to be gun-shy.

And you won't be stuck alone when I run off with that green-eyed hunk—the kids stay with you.''

"Some mother you are," Pat chided, his blue eyes sparkling as brightly as his wife's. "Denying your children the chance to live on another planet."

A chorus of "Another planet?" broke out and Adrienne groaned as all eyes turned to her. At that moment she was extremely grateful that Kendrick wasn't there to see her wring her eldest sister's neck. She gave Rosie a narrow-eyed glare. "You just couldn't keep that quiet, could you?"

Rosie shrugged sheepishly. "It kinda slipped out. Sorry."

The entire story of Adrienne's close encounter of the third kind soon "slipped out", dramatically embellished by Pat until everyone was hooting with laughter—everyone but Adrienne. She was seriously considering fratricide.

"I knew if I lived long enough, Addie'd pay for all those times she put a damper on my love life," Arnie inserted.

"You mean going to a space flick at the drive-in with the little sister in the back seat wasn't your idea of a perfect date?" Karen's husband, John, asked in mock sincerity. "I loved all the times I got to take her along."

Several wadded napkin balls hit him in the face.

For several minutes, the brothers-in-law tried to outdo each other with graphic descriptions of the torture they'd suffered as a result of Adrienne's chaperoning. "You mean you were after my body?" Josie cut in sharply.

"Damned right!" Arnie shouted lustily. "I almost died from those cold showers."

"Gosh fellas, if I'd had any idea sending Addie along with you would have caused so many cases of pneumonia, I never would have done it," Jerome Castle apologized, tongue in cheek.

"You sent her on purpose, Jerry Castle, and you know it," Rebecca reminded, confirming the suspicions of her sons-in-law.

After the jeers and the barrage of napkin balls stopped, the patriarch of the family admitted, "I had your numbers, boys. Now, which one of you big lugs is going to volunteer to chaperone my baby?"

The "hulk" was the obvious choice. "Not me, guys." Jim held up his hands. "I'm not tangling with some extraterrestrial superman. The princess is on her own with that green-skinned, laser-eyed wonder."

Adrienne reached the limit of her endurance as she suffered through another round of laughter and ridiculous suggestions. "Now look, you guys," she pronounced, coming to her feet. "This has gone on long enough. I want a promise from every one of you that you'll keep your mouth shut about this alien business when Kendrick gets here. He's as human as any of you!"

Her tirade was cut short as a loud whirring noise sounded from above, drawing everyone's attention to the sky. A helicopter appeared over the rooftops and then hovered over the back yard. A loud, ethereal voice boomed, "Give up the earthling woman called Adrienne."

Mouths that hadn't yet dropped open did when a gleaming silver figure emerged from the copter's doorway and began a smooth descent to the ground. No one moved, not even the children, as they watched the creature's descent. "Oh, no!" Adrienne moaned.

She'd never live this down. How could Kendrick do this to her after all she'd just said in his defense?

She was about to appeal to her mother but Rebecca Castle was grinning wildly. "Jerry, I told you he was perfect for Addie," she shouted over the roar of the whirling rotor blades.

Jerome Castle boomed with laughter, "Addie's found her knight on a white charger, don't you think?"

No one came to Adrienne's rescue as Kendrick landed on the ground and clumsily stalked her, the thick support line to his "mother ship" still attached and trailing behind him. "Come with me earthling," he ordered, his voice sounding hollow and eerie from within the confines of his helmet. He held out his gloved hand to her.

Adrienne hesitated a second too long. The silver creature emitted several loud beeps then promptly scooped her up and tossed her over his shoulder. He marched straight to Jerome and said, "Sir, I wish to marry this female. I promise to love her, care for her and grant her as many trips back to earth as she wishes."

"She's all yours," Jerome granted gaily, mopping the tears of laughter from his blue eyes.

Kendrick then turned toward Rebecca. "Ma'am, how quick can you plan a wedding?"

Brown eyes as soft and warm as her youngest daughter's expressed Rebecca's joy as she gazed through the visor to the man within. Without hesitation, she returned, "One week'll do it if you can whip up a tux by then."

"Can do," Kendrick promised, then asked, "Two-thirty earth time?"

"Don't I have anything to say about this?" Adrienne shouted, trying to wiggle into a more comfortable position on Kendrick's shoulder.

"Certainly dear," Rebecca allowed. "Which one of your sisters do you want as your matron of honor and would you like me to cut down the family wedding gown for you?"

"I haven't agreed to anything yet," Adrienne bellowed then squealed for help as she and Kendrick were lifted off the ground and began a slow ascent.

But as soon as she was installed safely in the copter, Adrienne did agree—or she tried to. Kendrick couldn't hear her over the roar of the motor.

Kendrick unfastened his helmet and lifted it from his head. "You what?" he bellowed.

"I said I'll marry you, you crazy creature. Blue eye, green eye, beepers, green skin and silver scales. You're the one I've been looking for all my life." She stopped and stared curiously at his head. She reached toward him and plucked at the curling, damp hair that hugged his scalp. "So that's why your hair looked so slimy."

"What?"

"The night we met, I thought you had slimy, green hair, but it was the lampshade and good, old-fashioned sweat. That getup must be hot."

"Only the helmet," he said. "The rest of the suit is quite comfortable. Now, shut up and give me your hand."

Adrienne slipped her hand in his but didn't follow his first command. "Maybe you should invent some little fan or cooling coils for your headgear," she suggested. "I'm going to quit my job and help you invent things. I've got lots of ideas. With your brain and my marketing skills, we'll take the patent office by storm.''

"Earth to Adrienne, earth to Adrienne," Kendrick pleaded, knowing she was drifting off on a tangent.

"Oh, Kendrick," she gasped in awe as he slipped a ring on her finger.

A brilliant-cut diamond, flanked by an emerald on one side and a sapphire on the other, sparkled on her hand. "Where in the world—" she started to ask then stopped herself. "I don't care where. It's beautiful." She looked up at him with eyes that glittered as brightly as the gems on her slender finger. "You're beautiful."

"That's my line and I adore you," he said, reaching for her.

"Your little girl was a beautiful bride," Dovie Hubbard complimented, dabbing a tear from the corner of her eye with a lace-edged hanky.

"Thank you, Dovie," Rebecca Castle responded, blowing her nose lightly into an identical handkerchief, gifts from the bride. "Kendrick was as handsome a groom as any we've had in this garden. Already he's as dear to me as the other sons my daughters have brought home."

Dovie beamed with a mother's pride. "He's a good man and he'll be good to your daughter," she vowed. "Couldn'ta picked a better wife for him if I'da gone lookin' myself."

The two women rocked contentedly in the comfortable chairs on the porch, gazing across the littered yard, not seeing the overturned folding chairs and straggling crepe paper, but the splendid scene enacted there hours before. Adrienne, lovely in the ivory satin gown that her mother and all her sisters had worn, and Kendrick, resplendent in a white tux, had repeated their vows beneath a flower-covered canopy before the loving assemblage of family and friends.

Karen, the only Castle sister not to have had the privilege before, had served as Adrienne's matron of honor. Greg Robinson had stood proudly beside Kendrick as his best man. As he'd done five times before, Jerome ceremoniously handed a daughter to a handsome man whose eyes were filled with love for her alone.

Jerome had kissed his daughter then turned away, smiling across the table at the shy, quiet couple from a West Virginia mountaintop who had come to witness the happiness of a man they had taken into their hearts. Taking a seat beside his wife, he reached for her hand and together they watched their youngest pledge herself in marriage. As the ceremony went on, they remembered the six pretty little girls who had played in the yard and grown up in the large frame house, and how eventually each in turn found her prince. Today's open declaration of love and devotion had closed one chapter of living but opened another.

Dovie smiled at the woman sharing the porch with her. "It was a grand wedding. I only wish Hattie May Carson had been here to see it. That would've put a stop to all her talk about haints. What Kendrick and Adrienne have together is real, the most human emotion there is—love."

Rebecca giggled. "Their love is real. But if I know my daughter, Hattie May will have plenty to talk about for years to come."

Far away in a magical room in a castle on Hubbard Mountain, Adrienne and Kendrick lay exhausted and replete on their bed. Each morning, they'd awakened to a celebration of color but now they lay in shadowy darkness. The love shining in each look and caress they offered each other was all the magic needed to brighten the room.

"Mrs. Sloan, do you expect all our children to be blond?" Kendrick asked, propping himself up on one elbow and dropping a quick kiss on his bride's pert little nose.

"Probably," Adrienne murmured, drawing a fingertip across Kendrick's lips. "Despite all laws of heredity, that blond gene in the Castle family seems to dominate." She trailed her finger down his throat, circled his Adam's apple then walked her fingers down his chest. "Arnie and Larry have hair almost as black as yours but their kids are all blond. Before Dad turned gray, his hair was black but look at us."

"How about height?" Kendrick inquired, his lips moving across her forehead then forging a path to her temple and down to her ear.

Adrienne squirmed when Kendrick's tongue circled the sensitive lobe. "Mmm, probably all tall. You're tall, my family's all tall except for me and Grandma Fruth."

"That sweet little lady who called me Mork?" he asked against the curve of her neck and shoulder.

"Oooh, that Rosie! She even told Grandma."

With Kendrick's hand skimming along her side and his tongue flicking her nipples to peaks, Adrienne had trouble holding onto any ill feeling toward her sister. Her mind was rapidly becoming occupied by her husband's arousing touch as he kissed his way down her body.

He tantalized her navel with his tongue until she was gasping for mercy. Abruptly, he raised his head and looked into her face. "Wow! We're going to have a whole colony of tall, blond, heterochromeairides right here on Hubbard's Mountain," he announced, levering himself over her and bracing most of his weight on his forearms.

The press of him against her softness made her catch her breath before asking, "Heterochromeairides?" A tiny niggle of suspicion knitted her brows as she gazed up at him.

"My brother was one, too. It must run in my family." Then he chuckled, recognizing her wide-eyed expression. "Different colored irises, darling. Remember?" He settled between her silken thighs and brushed his lips across hers.

"Then our children might have eyes like yours?"

"Mmm," he murmured against her lips. "Eyes and . . . We'll discuss their ears later. Much later," he vowed and took her mouth, issuing a fiery invitation to fly with him on a torrid journey beyond the restraints of earth.

Ears? Adrienne experienced only a second of concern then joined Kendrick in flight, knowing she could face anything as long as he was with her.

Silhouette Desire

Silhouette Desire Romances

TAKE 4
THRILLING SILHOUETTE
DESIRE ROMANCES
ABSOLUTELY FREE

Experience all the excitement, passion and pure joy of love. Discover fascinating stories brought to you by Silhouette's top selling authors. At last an opportunity for you to become a regular reader of Silhouette Desire. You can enjoy 6 superb new titles every month from Silhouette Reader Service, with a whole range of special benefits, a free monthly Newsletter packed with recipes, competitions and exclusive book offers. Plus information on the top Silhouette authors, a monthly guide to the stars and extra bargain offers.

**An Introductory FREE GIFT for YOU.
Turn over the page for details.**

As a special introduction we will send you FOUR
specially selected Silhouette Desire romances
— yours to keep FREE — when you complete
and return this coupon to us.

At the same time, because we believe that you will be so thrilled
with these novels, we will reserve a subscription to Silhouette
Reader Service for you. Every month you will receive 6 of the very
latest novels by leading romantic fiction authors, delivered direct to
your door.

Postage and packing is always completely
free. There is no obligation or commitment —
you can cancel your subscription at any time.

It's so easy. Send no money now. Simply fill in and post
the coupon today to:-

**SILHOUETTE READER SERVICE, FREEPOST,
P.O. Box 236 Croydon, SURREY CR9 9EL**

Please note: READERS IN SOUTH AFRICA to write to:-

**Independent Book Services P.T.Y.,
Postbag X3010, Randburg 2125, S. Africa**

FREE BOOKS CERTIFICATE

**To: Silhouette Reader Service, FREEPOST, PO Box 236,
Croydon, Surrey CR9 9EL**

Please send me, Free and without obligation, four specially selected Silhouette Desire Romances and reserve a
Reader Service Subscription for me. If I decide to subscribe, I shall, from the beginning of the month following my
free parcel of books, receive six books each month for £5.94, post and packing free. If I decide not to subscribe I
shall write to you within 10 days. The free books are mine to keep in any case. I understand that I may cancel my
subscription at any time simply by writing to you. I am over 18 years of age.
Please write in BLOCK CAPITALS.

Name _____

Address _____

_____

_____ Postcode _____

SEND NO MONEY — TAKE NO RISKS

*Remember postcodes speed delivery. Offer applies in U.K. only
and is not valid to present subscribers. Silhouette reserve the right
to exercise discretion in granting membership. If price changes
are necessary you will be notified.
Offer limited to one per household. Offer expires July 31st
1986.*

EP18SD